THE GALACTIC MI TEAM . . .

Captain Joshua Price—commanding officer, under-cover operative, anthropologist. He didn't always like what the Galactic MI team had to do to find the answers his superiors wanted—but he knew how to get them . . . no matter what the cost.

Lt. Emma Coollege—call her "Jackknife." Re-sourceful, fearless, a born survivor. She's the team's on-the-spot expert at everything from weapons to disguises. She's willing to break every rule in the book to get the job done—and she *always* gets the job done.

Master Sgt. Wallace ("Rocky") Stone—tough and deadly, a career soldier. He volunteered for a combat unit so he could be where the action was. But when he found out about Galactic MI, he switched—to get into the *real* action.

Highly trained intelligence agents who put their lives on the line for Earth—on alien worlds where death awaits the unwary!

**Don't miss the next book
in Kevin Randle's
new *GALACTIC MI* series,
The Rat Trap.
Coming soon from Ace Books**

GALACTIC MI

KEVIN RANDLE

ACE BOOKS, NEW YORK

This book is an Ace original edition,
and has never been previously published.

GALACTIC MI

An Ace Book / published by arrangement with
the author

PRINTING HISTORY
Ace edition / June 1993

ISBN: 0-441-27238-X

Ace Books are published by The Berkley Publishing Group,
200 Madison Avenue, New York, NY 10016.
The name "ACE" and the "A" logo
are trademarks belonging to Charter Communications, Inc.

PRINTED IN THE UNITED STATES OF AMERICA

10 9 8 7 6 5 4 3 2 1

CHAPTER

1

The mud-spattered alley was dark, the gray-green of the tiny moon hanging near the horizon doing little to illuminate the area. Joshua Price, known to his friends as Tree, stood at the entrance, but didn't enter. That seemed to be an invitation to death.

"Come on, you coward," said a harsh voice hidden in the shadows. "Come on."

Price reached down and felt the knife concealed along his thigh. A thin blade, razor-sharp, designed for only one thing and that was killing an enemy. He took a small step forward, wondering why it was necessary to find the man in the dark alley. Why not in one of the honky-tonks behind them. Music spilled out into the night making it difficult to hear. The light from the windows and doors did little to chase the gloom away, and someone had shattered each of the street lamps as if wanting the night to be extra dark.

"You want it, come on. I ain't got all night."

Price took a deep breath and forced himself deeper into the alley. He thought there were others around him, hidden

1

in the dark, but that was just a sense, an impression, or maybe it was fear. He swallowed audibly and walked toward the big man at the far end.

"You got the dough?"

"Here," said Price, touching his pocket. "Right here."

"Get it out and you get the holo."

"How do I know you're giving me the right holo?"

"Because I'm just going to take the money without counting it. I trust you. You trust me."

Price stopped in a deep shadow. Although the night was cool and dry, he felt the sweat bead and drip. He wanted to wipe it from his forehead but was afraid the movement would reveal his fear.

"Cube's right here," said the man. "Everything you could want. Right here."

Before Price could respond, there was a sudden blast of hot air and the quiet whine of an engine overhead. Bright light flared, pinpointing the rough-looking man. He raised a hand to shield his eyes, but he was looking at Price. "You brought the pigs."

"No . . . I need the cube."

"Fuck you. You let them follow. You're an asshole." His right hand stabbed into his slash pocket.

Price retreated, trying to pull his knife, knowing that it would be no good against a gun. He'd played it too fast and loose.

From overhead a voice said, "You are under arrest for treason. Drop your weapons and remain motionless with your hands up."

"You asshole," shouted the man again. He pulled his gun clear and aimed it at Price's chest.

Price ducked to one side and closed his eyes, knowing there was nothing he could do. He waited for the sudden, searing pain, aware of the quiet hum from the aircraft, the odor of the air, and the breeze on his face.

A single red beam stabbed out from above and touched the man on the top of the head. It winked out immediately and the man toppled into the mud without screaming. The gun dropped from his hand.

"Stand up," the voice commanded Price.

Price did as he was told and then looked at the body. The holo cube was still clutched in his left hand. Without thinking, Price darted forward, grabbed it, and then sprinted into the shadows.

"Halt or I'll shoot!"

Price dodged left and then right, turning a corner and running along the shadows. He jammed the holo into a pants pocket and struggled to unbutton his shirt. He slid to a halt, his back against the rough wood of a building, and stripped off the top shirt. He was aware of the hover car searching for him, the light probing the shadows.

He didn't know what kind of sensors they might have on the hover car. Maybe they didn't need the light to find him. Maybe they already knew where he was. Maybe they were toying with him for the fun of it.

But he couldn't stop. He turned and yanked at the door, which opened quietly. He ran through the building, down a long, narrow hall, and entered a large room. He crossed to the window and opened it, climbing out. The hover car was somewhere behind him. To the right was open country and to the left the edge of town.

Without thinking, Price ran to the left, turned a corner, and found himself staring into the face of a young woman. She grinned at him and asked the question that had been asked a thousand times before. "You want a date?"

It was called protective coloration. The instructors had stressed it throughout training. Blend in. Look as if you belong. With the girl on his arm, he was no longer the single man the police were pursuing. He was part of a couple and might be overlooked.

"You don't look so good," she said.

"I was . . . I just completed a big deal. Sucked the life out of me." Forcing a grin, he said, "But I'm looking to party now. Party hardy."

"You came to the right place." She tugged at his arm, dragging him into the closest bar.

It was crowded, noisy, and smoke-filled. Outworlders still smoked. There was a huge mirror behind the bar, two men working there, and a gigantic stock of liquor stacked near them. Music pounded, the beat heavy and maddening, but one woman danced to it, tossing bits of clothing into the shouting audience as the mood moved her.

The woman with Price leaned close and shouted at him, "I want a beer."

"Good," said Price. He shouldered his way through the mob at the bar and waited until one of the men looked at him. He ordered, received two mugs, and worked his way back to the woman, dodging the others who seemed too preoccupied to notice anything around them.

The music died a moment later and the interior was filled with flashing red lights. Three men in body armor, silver helmets, and power pistols pushed their way in. They waited near the door until the bar was silent.

"One man. Might have come in here four, five minutes ago. Where is he?"

A bartender said, "No one came in here."

"No one?"

He pointed at Price and the woman and said, "Just them. Bought a beer."

Price took a deep pull, swallowing the icy liquid as shards of pain danced behind his eyebrows. He wanted it to look as if he'd been drinking for more than a few seconds.

One of the men walked through the crowd that parted easily for him. He stared at Price, at his shirt, and then at the woman with him. His eyes were locked on Price's, waiting. Then, without a word, he whirled and joined the others.

As they exited, the woman said, "What was that all about?"

Price grinned and was about to tell her to get lost when it occurred to him that the police might be waiting for him outside. If he emerged without the woman, they'd grab him.

Of course, they might do it anyway, but with the woman his chances, for the moment, were better.

The music started abruptly, the lights near the raised stage began to flash, and the dancer tore off the last of her clothes. Price pulled his date close, the comforting weight of the knife against his thigh and the holo cube in his pocket. For the moment he was convinced that it didn't get any better.

It was two hours later that he saw a burly man enter, walking straight to the bar without looking to either side. He slammed a ham-sized fist down and demanded to be served. As he got his drink, he turned, leaning back, his elbows on the bar. He nodded to Price and then exited.

Price left the woman sitting at a table, telling her he'd be right back. He followed the man out into the night, saw him as he stepped off the sidewalk and into the shadow.

"You get it?" asked the man.

Price stepped close and nodded. "I got it."

"You missed the rendezvous."

"Thought it would be better if I stayed where I was. I figured someone would be along."

"Give it."

Price dug the cube out of his pocket and handed it over. "You'll see that it gets into the right hands?"

"Sure. You just go back in there."

Price shook his head. "No reason now. The cube has been passed."

"Right." He slipped back, deeper into the shadows, and then vanished.

Price stood there for a moment, trying to figure out his next move, and then heard a voice behind him. "You're under arrest. Turn slowly."

Price couldn't help laughing. They had found him just a little too late. The information had been passed. Raising his hands, he said, "What can I do for you?"

Price sat at the interrogation table feeling tired and dirty, but not frightened. He knew the local customs well and believed that they would try to scare him into confessing; they might engage in a little physical abuse but his superiors knew where he was and they would be trying to get him free quickly.

The planet wasn't a wealthy one, on the back flight routes where the decaying freighters called sporadically. Had they not been on the galactic rim, he would never have been there. Someone with more rank and more experience would have been brought in. His bosses had not concerned themselves with the danger, only that it was a nothing mission that would get no recognition unless it went terribly wrong. Then he would be dead and blamed and his bosses would be promoted eventually.

The interrogation room was small with a single table, three chairs, and a huge mirror that was obviously one-way glass. They had to be standing on the other side of it watching him to see if he was nervous. The worst thing he could do was look as if he was frightened. At the moment there was nothing to do other than sit quietly.

The door opened and a huge man walked in. His jet-black hair was plastered down, looking as if he'd just stepped from the shower. But the body odor that suddenly filled the room said that he hadn't bathed in a long time.

Price chose to ignore that and said, "I don't belong here. You have arrested the wrong man and if I'm not allowed to contact my boss, there'll be hell to pay."

The big man jerked one of the chairs around, plopped it down, and then sat. He stared at Price, grinned with broken teeth, and said, "We've got a picture of you robbing the body of a dead man."

"No, you've got a picture of me retrieving an item that belonged to me."

"Where is it?"

"What?"

"The holo cube you took from the dead man."

Price took a deep breath and rubbed the back of his neck. "I gave it to a friend."

"Then you'd better call him and get it back."

For the first time, Price began to worry. There was no way to recall the cube. It was off planet already, probably being analyzed as they spoke. He could no more call the man than he could fly out of the room.

"I'm not shitting you, sonny. That cube had better reappear in the next few minutes or you're not walking out of here. Not ever."

"A call," said Price. "I need to make a call but I don't know the number. That woman . . ."

"What woman?"

"I met her at the bar. I slipped the cube into her purse when she wasn't looking. She has it and doesn't know it."

The big man laughed. He threw his head back and laughed loud and long. "You think we're so incompetent that we don't have her under arrest. She has been searched, her purse has been searched, and she had nothing."

"Neither do I," said Price.

The big man stood up and towered over Price. The room was filled with menace. Raising his voice, he said, "You're not going to walk out of here until we have some answers. Until we learn what you did with the cube."

Price looked down at the table and then pulled at a splinter on the edge of it. He was aware of the man standing over him, almost breathing on him, but he wanted it to appear that he didn't care.

"What did you do with the cube?"

"I threw it away. It wasn't going to do me any good. I got rid of it."

"You passed it to someone."

Price's head snapped up and he realized that he could have said he'd given it to anyone in the bar. Now it was too late for that. If he began to change his story now, it would be a tip-off.

"We have a cell so far back that no one goes there. Sunlight never reaches there. You could spend the rest of your very short life there."

A tap at the door caught the officer's attention and he turned, reaching out to open it. There was a whispered conversation and the man shouted, "Fuck that!" The conversation resumed and then ended abruptly.

"Okay, smart ass, someone has posted bail for you. Seems that stealing the cube from a dead man is not a major offense . . . I think you should rot until you help. See the sergeant at the desk."

Price knew that it had to be a trick, but he wasn't going to ignore the opportunity to get out. It was the opening he needed to get clear.

As he reached the door, the man grabbed him and spun him around. With his face only inches away, he said, "You'd better be very careful. I'm going to be watching you, and you make one little mistake, you're a dead man."

"Sure," said Price. He spoke quietly and carefully, trying not to offend the big man. It was the last thing he wanted to do. Not with freedom staring him in the face.

"I'll be very careful."

CHAPTER 2

Of course Price recognized the woman who had bailed him out. She was a tall woman, just a fraction under six feet, slender with light brown hair when she allowed her natural color to show. Her features were delicate, almost classical, but she could disguise them easily, the disguises fooling even Price. Here she was dressed as a planet native, the colors of her coverall rather drab. It did nothing to mask her beauty and that explained the hovering crowd of police who wanted to help her if they could.

Price walked to the window where an officer stood with a manila envelope. He handed it to Price and said, ''Check the contents and then sign this receipt.''

Price spilled the contents onto the countertop, made a swift count of the cash. ''There's some missing.''

''You want to file a complaint, you see the captain in the morning. You don't want to sign the receipt, we keep the stuff and you can pick it up in the morning.''

''Come on,'' said the woman. ''Let's get out of here.''

Price ran a hand through his short hair and then wiped it

on the front of his shirt. He grabbed the receipt, scrawled his signature on it, and shoved it back.

The officer smiled broadly and said, ''Thank you so much for your cooperation. Have a nice day.''

The woman took Price's hand and pulled him toward the door. As soon as they were outside, she said, ''You almost blew it in there.''

''My foot, Emma.''

''How much money did they take? Couldn't have been all that much, and besides, you'll be reimbursed for any loss.''

''I don't say something and they get more suspicious.''

She rolled her eyes at heaven. ''As if that would make any difference.'' She dragged him down the steps. ''Let's just get the hell out of here.''

They reached the street and she opened the door of a car, climbing in behind the wheel. She waited as Price hurried around to the passenger side. As soon as he closed the door, she started the engine and they came up to a hover.

Over the roar of the turbine, she said, ''We're getting the hell off this planet. Things are breaking down too quickly.''

''I'm going to jump bail?''

''Those are the orders,'' she said. She glanced to the rear and then pulled out, into the center of the driving lane. The headlights danced across the short grass.

''You know they're going to follow us,'' said Price.

''Of course. They think you'll head to your hideout and there they'll find the cube.''

''But Stone has it.''

''Stone has it,'' she confirmed. ''Or had it. He should have passed it on by now.''

Price twisted around in the seat and looked back, over his shoulder. The sidewalk and street were empty. The police building—a massive structure of stone, steel, and glass—was brightly lit. There was no movement near it. No cars suddenly on the street by it.

''Looks clear,'' said Price.

''They're back there. Believe me,'' she said.

Price turned around and focused his attention on the road in front of them. They had moved to the outskirts of the city where the resident halls were long and low and older. The streetlights were few and far between.

As they pulled out on a straightaway, she said, "If there's anyone back there, we'll spot them now."

Price didn't bother to turn. He looked up at the rearview mirror and then at the side mirror, but there was no lights in them. "Could be using choppers."

"Yeah, I suppose." She slowed.

"This thing has been bad from the first minute we set foot on the planet."

"Almost out now."

Price closed his eyes momentarily, but could only see the big, dirty man being hit by the beam, dropping into the mud of the alley. Not a good way to die. He hadn't been an evil man, just an opportunist.

"What was that?"

"Where?"

She had ducked slightly and was trying to see out of the top of the windshield. "Thought something flew over the top of us."

"You heading directly to the spaceport?"

"Why not?"

"If they are following, they could stop us there. I think we'd better slow down and make a turn like we're heading back into town." He tugged at the sleeve of his shirt so that he could see the glowing numbers of his watch. "Bars will be having last call about now."

"I don't like it, Tree."

"Just do it."

"Nicks is waiting at the spaceport. Everything is set. We can be lifting off within a minute of arriving."

Price thought about that. Everything finished in a minute. Someone else in charge, making the decisions. That had appeal. Of course, it would do no good if the police were alerted and had a ship in low orbit to intercept. They might be on standby, especially with them making a beeline to the spaceport.

"Let's head for the bars."

She shot him a glance and then shrugged. "Sure. If you think that's best."

Price settled back into the seat and let the scenery flash by him. He'd walked along the streets a dozen times, spoken to the people, shopped in the stores, and lived in a two-room apartment that was available by the hour, day, or week, hidden away in a part of the city never visited by the citizens. It was a self-imposed cage that was allowed to exist to keep the troublemakers away from the rest of society. He'd tired to maintain a low profile there but apparently someone had noticed.

"It would be good to get off this mudball," said Price, "just as quickly as possible."

"That's what I've been trying to tell you."

The bright lights appeared in the distance. Price pointed and said, "Pull over. Let's get out."

She steered to the side and let the car settle to the ground. She switched off the engine and then pushed on the door, forcing it open.

Before he got out, Price said, "You have anything of a personal nature in here?"

"What? No."

"Good. Let's go."

As Price came around the car, he took her hand. Lowering his voice, he said, "Emma, we've got to get clear. The car is too easy to follow."

"We're ten miles from the spaceport."

"Relax."

Together they walked across the street and then entered one of the bars. The music and talk was so loud that it hurt the ears. No one seemed to be speaking in a normal tone of voice. A bottle flashed through the air and shattered against the wall, but the din overwhelmed the sound.

"What the hell?" asked Emma.

"Just follow me," said Price. He shouldered his way through the crowd, ignoring the looks of the strangers. He approached the short hall that led to the bathrooms and worked his way down it. There was an emergency exit there, blocked by a stack of broken-down chairs.

"Great," she said. "Violation of the fire code."

Hitchhiking a thumb over his shoulder, Price asked, "You want to go tell the owner?"

"No."

Price began to peel the stack away from the door, piling the chairs along the wall. When he finished, he pushed on the door, but it refused to open. He put a shoulder into it and shoved again, and when that failed, he took a step back.

"What are you going to do?"

"Watch." He kicked once, striking the door close to the knob. It burst open. Price grabbed Emma's hand and dragged her out into the night. As soon as he was outside, he slammed the door shut again and then flattened himself against the side of the building.

"What are we doing?"

"If they have a chopper in the air, the observer might have seen a flash of light when the door opened. He might drift around here and that'll give us a chance to spot him."

"Oh."

Price scanned the night sky. There were no clouds to obscure the bizarre star patterns. They weren't far enough from Earth for all the familiar constellations to be gone, but enough of them had changed to look distorted, as they might have a hundred thousand years earlier on Earth. The gray-green moon had climbed higher into the sky but it was a small, dim object, not at all like the moon of Earth.

Price searched for a black shape against the charcoal night, but nothing appeared. If the police had a chopper up and searching, it hadn't been alerted when the door opened.

"We're still ten miles from the spaceport."

"I know that. Just stay close to me now. We've got to make some time."

With that Price ran across the open field behind the building, reaching a short wooden wall. He stopped at the base of it, searched the sky overhead, and then reached up, grabbing the top. He hauled himself up, and slipped a leg over. He took another look and then dropped to the ground.

As soon as Emma joined him, he ran along the fence, staying close, using the shadows. He was aware of the sounds coming from the bars that lined the street. Music and noise filled the night. There were shouts and what sounded as if a fight was taking place.

When they reached the end of the alley, Price dropped to one knee. He poked his head out into the street but there was little traffic now that it was almost dawn.

"It'll take hours to get to the spaceport," Emma said.

"Not if we steal a car." He pointed. "Like that one right over there."

She had to laugh. "I've just bailed you out and now we're going to steal a car."

"And park it at the spaceport. The owner will probably be too drunk to notice it's gone."

"Sure."

Price got to his feet, his back against the rough wood of the fence. He took a deep breath and then stepped out onto the street. He walked toward the car with great care, exaggerating his movements to imitate a drunk who knew that he'd had too much but was trying to fool others. Near the middle of the street he staggered slightly and then straightened. With great dignity, he tugged at the tail of his shirt as if to straighten it, and then continued on. At the car, he patted his pockets as if searching for the keys and then reached down for the door handle. It opened under the slightest pressure.

Price scrambled inside, ducked down, and pulled at the wires under the dashboard. He stripped two of them away, touched them together, and heard the turbine begin to whine. He wrapped the wires together, surprised that the simple hot-wiring would work. Most of the newer cars had antithief ignitions.

As the car came up on the cushion of air, he leaned out the door and waved at Emma. She ran across the street and climbed on board.

"Spaceport in about ten minutes, if everything goes right," he said.

"Good."

He spun the wheel and the craft turned on its axis. As it did, he saw the black shape of a helicopter in the sky above the street.

"I think they found us."

"Let's just get the hell out of here."

Price knew that the police would be able to guess the destination, but the time was becoming critical. They had to escape. He pushed forward slightly, felt the nose of the vehicle dip, and they began to pick up speed.

"You're not going to try to outrun them, are you?"

"The chopper could climb to fifteen thousand feet and watch the whole city. No way to outrun it."

"So what are you going to do?"

Keeping his attention focused on the dark road, Price said, "Head to the spaceport."

"We could have done that an hour ago."

"Maybe." He leaned forward, turned his head to see out of the top of the windshield. He searched the sky, noticing that it was beginning to brighten slightly. He could not see the chopper.

"Look behind us," he said. "See if you can spot that chopper."

Emma turned and got up on her knees, hanging over the back of her seat and trying to see out the rear window. "I don't see it anywhere around."

"Then I'm going right to the spaceport."

They rode in silence, away from the lights of the bars and taverns contained in the small "combat" zone, toward the quieter residential area, through it, and out into the open country. Ahead was the orange glow of the spaceport.

As they approached the perimeter fence, Price said, "Looks like we're going to make it."

They passed through the open gate, turned to the right, and followed the designated route toward the main terminal buildings.

"Nicks should be waiting by the cargo port," said Emma.

Price slowed and turned toward the parking area. It was nearly deserted and the lighting around it poor. One man wandered around it aimlessly as if he had no place to go.

"What are you doing?"

"We're here. Let's walk now."

As the car settled and Price shut down the turbine, Emma leaned into her door and forced it open. She stepped out and dropped to the ground.

Price followed suit and then looked up, into the charcoal sky. The stars had faded with the coming of the sun. Nowhere around them was a sign of the chopper.

"I think we made it," said Emma.

"That was too easy."

She said, "Let's go," and started toward the cargo port.

Overhead was the feathery whisper of a bird in flight. Price stopped and looked up at the police helicopter as it dropped to a hover twenty-five feet over him.

Emma kept moving, jogging ahead of him. She slowed, glanced back, and then stopped.

"Run!" yelled Price.

An amplified voice boomed from the chopper. "You are under arrest for vehicle theft."

"Shit," said Price. He stood flat-footed, looking up at the aircraft, and then decided it was time to act. He spun and sprinted for the cargo area. He hurtled a short fence and then a living wall made of bush and vine. He crossed a pathway and ran for the corner of a hangar.

The nose of the chopper dropped and it slipped forward,

flying over him. The nose came up, and the chopper slowed, slipping toward the tarmac in front of the cargo port.

Emma slid to a stop, staring at the helicopter as a door opened and men began to leap out. They were all dressed in black, wore body armor, and carried rifles.

Price stopped suddenly, out of ideas. He dropped into a fighting crouch and knew it was useless. Unarmed combat only worked if the opponent was also unarmed. He stood up.

"Stand where you are," commanded the voice.

Price took a deep breath and felt the sweat begin to bead on his forehead. The sun was higher and the humidity of the day was beginning to build. It was going to be a boiler.

There was a flash from the right and the nose of the helicopter erupted into a fiery ball of orange. It dropped to the tarmac with a metallic crunch. The police officers dived for cover as a small craft whipped from the shadows at the rear of the hangar. The nose popped up and it dropped to the ground between Emma and Price. The small canopy flipped up and Nicks screamed, "Come on."

Price ran forward, stepped on the stubby wing, and leapt into the rear seat. Emma was a step behind him. He grabbed her hand, pulling her in. As she fell into his lap, the canopy closed and there was a roar from the engine. They lifted off from that point, the backblast searing a corner of a hangar and setting a pallet of cargo on fire.

The police officers reacted immediately, firing at the tiny craft. Their beams were absorbed and the energy dispersed into the atmosphere around them in tiny pops and miniature lightning bolts.

The shock of sudden acceleration forced them down into the soft seat. Price, his eyes open, could see beams flashing past the cockpit.

They passed through a cloud and the roar from behind lessened as the pressure lifted. Over his shoulder, Nicks shouted, "You two okay?"

"Fine," said Price. "Glad to see you."

"Same, sir."

CHAPTER

3

They climbed into the upper reaches of the atmosphere where the sky faded to a dull purple and then into a deep black. Price shifted around and struggled with his shoulder harness. When he buckled it, he said, "They'll be able to catch us."

"Nope," said Nicks. He pointed through the cockpit. "Here comes the cavalry."

"I see them."

"You two okay back there? I had to get us out kind of quick."

"I'm fine. Emma?"

"I think I strained a muscle in my back," she said. "I feel it tugging back there."

The other ship turned and it seemed as if it were drifting toward them slowly. The engines flared once and it rolled to the left. The two came close and a hatch on the side of the large one opened. Nicks nudged the controls, aimed at a light set at the far end of the shuttle bay, and let his ship drift into the interior. It touched the deck with a metallic click.

"We're home, children," said Nicks.

Price unbuckled his harness and let the straps float up and out of the way. The hatch on the ship closed, and the lights came up, first tinged with red and then yellow as the air was pumped back into the chamber.

When it was safe, Nicks opened the canopy and climbed out. He dropped to the deck and then waited as the other two got down.

"Colonel wants to see you as soon as possible," said Nicks. "Full uniform."

Price rubbed a hand on the whiskers and said, "He'll probably want me to shave too."

"Yes, sir."

"I take it from this that Stone got the cube off."

Nicks leaned forward and closed the canopy, latching it shut. He straightened and said, "Drone off within minutes of receiving it. No trouble there."

The three walked across the deck, toward the hatch. They ignored the control room set off to one side, a half-dozen other small penetration ships, the colored lights that flashed, and the technicians who were now entering for maintenance on their ship. There was no reception committee from the bridge or the command staff.

The hatch irised open and Price stepped through first, ducking down slightly. When the others had joined him, he said to Emma, "I guess we meet in the colonel's conference room in what . . . twenty minutes."

"Yes, sir."

Price and Emma walked down the corridor toward the visiting officers' quarters. It was a narrow corridor, dimly lighted. The bulkheads were smooth but there were some pipes and conduits running along the top, near the corners. The ship was a fast corvette, designed to skim the planet's atmosphere, dispatch small scout craft, and then retire at high speed.

They reached the end of the corridor where a small lift

would take them up or down, depending. Price stood to one side and said, "You first."

Emma caught the up link and disappeared. Price watched her go and then climbed on. She had headed to her temporary quarters when he reached the next level. Alone, he walked down the short corridor and touched the thumb-plate next to the door. It opened quietly and he stepped inside.

There was a small bunk that folded from the bulkhead. There was a chair bolted to the deck, a small desk, and a rack for uniforms. By flipping the desk around, top to bottom, it was transformed into a small sink with a trinkle of water. As Price stepped in front of it, a section of wall brightened and Price saw his reflection.

Price was a tall, thin man whose face was now hidden by a layer of dirt and the beginnings of a brown beard. Bright blue eyes stared back at him. After using his razor to scrape away the beard, he revealed his angular features and sharp chin. He decided that he had looked better in the beard, but military and space regulations prohibited them.

He bent down and splashed water onto his face. He straightened and dried himself. There wasn't time for a shower so he picked the oldest of his uniforms and put it on quickly. Satisfied, for the moment, he headed to the hatch.

He reached the conference room at the same time as Emma and Stone. He centered himself on the hatch and when it irised open, he stepped through. Without a word, he moved to a position along the table but didn't sit. When the others had joined him, he looked at the Colonel and said, "Sir, Captain Price, Lieutenant Coollege, and Sergeant Stone, reporting."

The Colonel was a small man with black hair, white skin, and brown eyes. He sat at the head of the table, a leather folder in front of him, next to the button controls for a variety of audiovisual equipment and displays. He looked up at once and then lifted a hand to return the salute. "Be seated."

When they sat, he leaned back and grinned. "That was well done, though the end was a little less than textbook."

"Thank you, sir. I hope it was worth it."

"Do any of you know what was on the cube?"

"No, sir," said Price. "The local police didn't seem to care too much about it."

"Not true. Monitoring suggests that they knew it was important. They took a calculated risk hoping to recover but failed."

"Yes, sir," said Price.

The Colonel touched a button near his left hand and a cloud of swirling light appeared just above the surface of the table. It flashed and popped and then solidified. A banner appeared above the display in bright green letters giving the time and date the holo had been made.

"We have, quite naturally, reviewed this whole thing carefully. As you'll see, our job is not done on the planet's surface."

The cube run was short, no more than three minutes. It appeared that someone had set a remote, placed it out of the way so that the field of view was slightly skewed as if it had been set low.

"That it?" asked Price.

"The relevant part."

"It doesn't make any sense," said Coollege.

"No, Emma, it doesn't."

"Which means we go back to the planet's surface," said Stone.

"Exactly, but not right away." The Colonel pointed at the center of the table where the last scene from the holo was held static, a frozen moment in time. "First, I want to discuss your impressions of that."

Coollege repeated, "It doesn't make any sense."

"What's wrong with it?" asked the Colonel.

Coollege leaned back but didn't say anything right away. "I guess I'm not sure."

"Okay. Analysis of the holo has provided us with the problem. We have what is supposed to be a native representative, from the first colonists to reach this planet, and a representative or an official of Earth. We don't like the looks of this. That meeting shouldn't have taken place. It was completely unauthorized."

Price was confused. "I thought everything had been consolidated into one massive, worldwide government. There are no natives, so to speak."

"The point is this. They have a fairly well regulated society down there." The Colonel touched another button and the display changed. A tiny man stood next to a small globe that displayed the planet's land masses and oceans. The industrial complexes, cities, communications centers, military and police facilities were all marked. "Let's listen to this quick briefing."

The voice of the tiny man filled the room. "Discovered as a virtual Earth duplicate without a sentient race, Bolton's Planet, designated M-234, was instantly colonized two hundred years ago. Government control was headquartered in New Washington and has been held there since."

A complete view of New Washington took over the center of the table, the man and his globe disappearing. "All things flow from the central computer complex that controls the various phases of daily life from what jobs one holds, to how many children a couple is authorized, and what goods and services are available to a specific individual."

"Sounds like the place should have been called New Beijing," said Stone.

"Hey, they have a system that works for them," said the Colonel.

". . . can currently field an army of about twenty thousand, a state police force of one hundred thousand men and women, and a network of counselors and therapists for the general population. Crime has been virtually eliminated and recreation is strictly monitored.''

"I guess,'' said Price.

''The only seemingly chaotic factor is a small area that was once termed a 'combat zone.' All bars, taverns, nightclubs, bordellos, and feely theaters are located in a highly regulated and strictly confined area. Off-world anthropologists believe the area is used to identify abnormal personalities in a sort of self-capture. The people are drawn to this area because of its publicized lawlessness. Society is protected as the people self-select themselves out of it. Eventually they are arrested and treated.''

Price nodded vigorously. ''I understand it now. We can't sneak onto the planet because of the computerization. That's why they had no trouble locating us.''

The Colonel touched the buttons and the display faded. ''Now we have an indication of a cooperation between that government and an unauthorized representative of Earth. This is one meeting that shouldn't have taken place.''

''Haven't you been able to listen to the conversation?'' asked Stone.

''They were using a noisemaker. Our people have been trying to filter out the noise, but it was well planned. Their voices drop down in the low-range frequencies and as we drop out those freqs, the voices fade out as well. Besides, they were speaking quietly.''

Price leaned forward and rubbed a hand through his hair. It was getting hard to think. He'd had almost no sleep in the last twenty-four hours and thoughts of bed kept intruding. ''We've every piece of equipment ever invented and we can't drop out a low-level vibration?''

The Colonel shrugged. ''Sometimes there are factors that just make no sense.''

Price took a deep breath. ''I don't see how we're going to penetrate this one.''

''Captain, let me tell you that there is a variety of information that we need before we can intervene in this planet's government. They are a sovereign government, duly constituted, and an associate member of the Coalition. We can't just land a brigade or two on our suspicions.''

''That didn't cut it?'' said Price, referring to the cube they had just seen.

''No.''

''Their reaction?'' asked Stone. ''They fired on the captain and the lieutenant as they tried to get out. That seems to be fairly hostile.''

''They fired on fleeing felons,'' said the Colonel matter-of-factly.

''We went into this,'' said Coollege, ''without a proper briefing.''

''That's why there will not be an immediate reinsertion. We have got to plan this a little better.''

''We need someone who was born down there or has lived down there. We need someone who can provide us with all the inside information,'' said Price.

The Colonel shifted through his folder and said, ''I have a series of orders here. Sergeant Stone, I'm going to want you and two others, of your own choice, to return to the planet and grab us a number of locals.''

Price laughed out loud. ''You just warn us about the sovereignty of the planet and then order one of my people to kidnap a local.''

''Small operations in the interest of peace and the stability of this region of space are authorized by the Coalition.'' The Colonel's voice had a hard edge to it.

''Yes, sir.''

''Now, once the prisoners have been delivered, I want you and Lieutenant Coollege to begin a complete interrogation of them. Learn everything you can about the society. Until then, the Anthropological Staff has put together an ethnology to give you some insight.''

''We should have done this before the reconnaissance,'' said Price.

"Looking at the results," said the colonel, "I believe that you might be right."

Stone broke in. "How soon do you want me to make planetfall?"

"End of the week."

"I can't just drop in. Not with the way they regulate those people."

"We have a diplomatic mission going down. You'll be attached to that as a cultural observer with the Coalition Anthropological Office."

Stone grinned. "Great. Who thought this up?"

"It allows you to roam around the streets as an observer. Gets you out of the office."

"Yes, sir."

The Colonel closed his folder and said, "I'll want to be kept apprised of the progress of the mission on a daily basis." He stood up.

The others stood quickly. Price said, "Yes, sir."

Without another word the Colonel moved to the hatch and let it open so that he could exit. He stepped through and turned quickly, giving them a half wave as it irised shut.

Price fell back in the chair. "I knew they had blown the recon when I stepped foot on that planet. Too much went wrong too quickly."

"We didn't do our homework," said Coollege.

"No, Emma, we weren't given the opportunity to do it. We assumed that the society was human normal and it wasn't. That was our mistake. We won't make it again."

Stone laughed. "And I have to become a kidnapper."

"Whatever." Price pushed on the edge of the table. "I say we meet at the lounge in about an hour."

Stone sprung to attention. "Yes, sir."

"Okay, Tree," said Coollege. "I'll see you in about an hour."

"This is getting weird again," said Price. "Real weird."

CHAPTER 4

They had slipped from close to Bolton's Planet to the outer reaches of the star system. They had transferred from the small shuttle ship to the larger command vessel where they were normally stationed. It was in a loose orbit around the star that was so far from them that it was just another bright point of light. A little bigger and brighter than any of the other stars, but a point of light nonetheless.

The lounge, more of a large conference room with chairs bolted to the floor but on swivels so that the occupants could either look out into the star-swept sky, or turn to face one another in conversation, was sparse. No more than twenty people could occupy the lounge at any one time. Since it was still midafternoon, ship's time, there were plenty of vacant seats.

Captain Joshua Price sat in the center chair, looking down at the disk of a frozen planet, its two moons in the sky behind it. A single outpost, on the north pole, served as a beacon to ships of commerce that entered the system, directing them toward Bolton's Planet. They were far enough from it that it had a faint orange cast to it, but might have been swirling snows refracting sunlight.

He felt a hand on his shoulder and turned. "Emma."

She dropped into the chair and said, "What are you doing?"

"Thinking."

"About?"

"Not all that much, really. I was just wondering what thought processes go on above us. At the higher staff levels. They drop us into an environment without the proper briefing, let us bull our way around for a day, and then seem surprised when we fail to accomplish everything."

Coollege was quiet for a moment, staring out into space. Now that they were back, now that they had been through the debriefing, as quick as it had been, she decided that she'd had enough. She didn't want to talk about the time below. At the moment she didn't even want to think about it.

She turned around and noticed that the lights near the bar were all off. No one would be there until after the end of the day shift. It prevented men and women from slipping from their duty stations to the lounge for a quick one when times were slow.

"So we're going back," she said finally, unable to think of anything else to say.

"Not before we understand what in the hell is going on down there. Part of military intelligence is having a complete file on the culture. Think of the trouble that could have been avoided in the past if the Army had understood the enemy. Really understood them."

Stone appeared carrying a small jug and three large glasses. He sat down, opened the jug, and poured three stiff drinks. He handed one to Coollege, one to Price, and then held up the third. "To us: the only people we can trust."

Price swallowed some of the alcohol in his glass and then coughed. He doubled over, set the remainder of his drink on the deck near his feet. Tears ran from his eyes. "What in the hell was that?"

"An experimental mix . . . I developed the formula myself. Brewed it up the main latrine."

"Ship's captain catches you," said Coollege, her voice suddenly husky, "and he'll have you keelhauled."

Stone rocked back in his chair, laced his fingers behind his head, and said, "That would be interesting to see, in space. I wonder if I'd get a suit."

"I don't think so," said Price.

"No, I suppose that would obscure the point," said Stone.

Master Sergeant Wallace Stone, called Rocky, was a short, dark man with dark brown eyes that were nearly obscured by his brow ridges and eyelids. It gave him a sleepy, nonthreatening look, especially since he was thin, nearly skinny. He had been in the Army for just over twenty years, had started as an infantry soldier, but his natural gift for languages and for creative thought had identified him early. Others had seen his potential, but he had resisted all change, wanting to stay in the infantry where he thought the action was. When he learned it was with the MI, he stopped protesting and allowed himself to be recruited. Although only a sergeant, he had masqueraded as a brigadier general on more than one occasion. It wasn't that he liked the benefits of the high rank, it was that he enjoyed playing a role so well that others couldn't see through it.

Suddenly serious, Stone said, "Sir, am I really going to have to kidnap someone?"

"Legal and political questions aside," said Price, "it looks as if you're going to have to do it."

"It's illegal," said Stone.

"Now there is an interesting question. Is it illegal when the government orders you to do it? The government is always ordering people to commit what would be crimes."

"I don't see this as a lawful order," said Stone. He held up a hand. "I know what you're going to say. We kill people all the time, but those are other soldiers trying to kill us. They are all combatants. A state of war exists between them and us. I can even make a case for unrestricted bombing, though I think surgical strikes into the heart of the enemy's industrial zones makes more sense than just dropping bombs on cities wholesale. But even then, a state of war exists. Now, suddenly, with no state of war, I'm ordered to the planet's surface to kidnap two people. It's not right.''

''Have you said anything to the Colonel?'' asked Price.

''No, sir. I figured to follow the chain of command. I'd mention it to you and see what you thought.''

Price picked up his glass, took a small drink, and then blew out as if he'd bitten into something too hot to chew. ''I think that we're dealing with a situation here that has no real legal answer. Government makes the laws and if the government decides that it is all right to kidnap, then I don't see a way around it.''

''The old U.S. Constitution had a provision about unlawful search and seizure. Doesn't this come under that heading?''

''Sergeant, you have a moral objection to this mission, right?''

''Yes, sir.''

''Then express it as a moral objection. You start arguing legal questions and they're going to be able to find precedence throughout human history and when all is said and done they'll tell you that sometimes individuals must be sacrificed for the greater good.''

''Shit.''

''Hey, I don't believe that,'' said Price. ''I guess I'm just trying to figure the rationalization going on.''

''I tell the Colonel that I object to the mission on moral grounds, what do you think he's going to say?''

Coollege, who had been quietly sipping at her drink, chimed in. ''Yeah. What's he going to say?''

''He's going to make it clear that there is no difference.

You have your orders and if you're not willing to carry them out, then you are in violation of them. I think he'll make it clear that you'll be court-martialed for failure to obey your orders. Even if you're not, you're going to find your career ruined."

"Shit, sir, what am I going to do?"

Price turned his attention to the sky outside the ship. In the far distance was a twinkling marking the location of the fleet. Thirty ships were there, all standing just outside the system, waiting to learn what was happening on the planet's surface and if they would be called to support action by an ambassador or if a military solution was necessary. That was why Price was there. To help make that determination.

Of course, learning everything they could was part of the job. The best way to learn about a culture was not to ride around in the air-conditioned hover car while officials pointed to only the things they wanted seen. The best way was to wander with the natives.

"You can look at it this way," said Price finally. "If you don't do it, someone else will. Your stand will do nothing to stop this mission at this time. However, if you participate, then you'll be in a better position to keep it from happening again. Besides, all we're going to do is talk to them about their society. They'll be returned as soon as the interrogation is finished."

Stone slammed a hand to the arm of his chair. "No, sir. It is not that simple."

"Rocky, there is nothing else I can tell you. You can either complete your mission or not. The choice is yours. At the moment, the lawful orders demand that you complete it. That's the key here. These are your lawful orders."

There was silence in the lounge for the next several minutes, the only sounds from the functioning of the ship and a quiet hum of the air-conditioning. Stone filled his glass again, drank deeply, and then set it back on the deck.

"If I do it," he said, "then I can make sure that the

people are protected. I can make sure that they are returned as soon as possible.''

Price looked at the older man. He knew that Stone was beginning to rationalize the next few days. Stone would complete the mission even though he didn't like it. His reason for doing it was that he could protect, to some extent, the victims. Price realized that he had talked Stone into it, and Price wasn't happy about it.

Stone stood up and then picked up his jug and the glasses. "I guess I'll be in my cube, if you want me, sir.''

"What about dinner?''

"No, sir. I don't think I'm up for dinner. I'll see you in the morning.''

When he was gone, Coollege said, "Sometimes I don't like this job very much.''

"Sometimes I agree with you.''

Price returned to the office, leaving Coollege in the lounge, standing with her back to the door, staring down at the tiny disk of the frozen planet. He entered the office, a small cabin with computer access to the ship's mainframe, the library computer on the admiral's flagship, and a variety of sensors and recording devices. He could learn practically everything he needed to know sitting at that console. There were two stations there and half a dozen screens.

He sat down at the desk, powered on the computer, and then checked the E-mail. Nothing other than routine reports had been logged in during his time dirtside. There were interesting after-action reports from other MI detachments, a report on the discovery of the inhabitable planet farthest from Earth, and a request from all personnel to submit ideas for the upcoming change in standard uniform.

Military organizations, like other giant bureaucracies, flowed on the make work and the ridiculous. Did the brass hats actually believe that the lower-ranking personnel cared about the design of another uniform? Everyone but the brass wanted everything left alone so that they wouldn't be required to make wholesale changes in their current inventory of uniforms.

Satisfied that everything was in order and there was nothing that he needed to do that minute, Price left the office, making sure to lock the hatch. His office was one of the few that required a lock. Even on ship there were men and women not authorized to know exactly what happened inside that cabin. The ship's captain could get in, but a record would be made of that entry and he would have to have a good reason for it.

Price returned to his cabin, figuring that he would just sack out. It had been a long day following a longer night. Sleep, rather than a huge meal, was what he needed. It was about all he could think about.

The quiet bong at the hatch caught him just as he was about to slip into sleep. For a moment he thought about ignoring it and then pushed himself up, flipped the bunk up, back into the bulkhead, and crossed to the hatch. He touched a button and let it iris open.

Coollege stepped through, looked at him, and asked, "Were you asleep?"

"Not quite. I was thinking about it, but hadn't quite made it."

She couldn't look him in the eye. She hesitated and then said, "Well, you asked Rocky to dinner but didn't say anything to me about dinner. I feel left out."

Price scratched the back of his head and frowned. "Rocky was upset."

"Well, so am I. I bailed you out of jail without so much as a thank you. I helped you steal a car and drove you to the spaceport. Now you don't want to have dinner with me. I could see this as discrimination. Major discrimination."

"I didn't know it meant that much to you."

"I think that's the problem. You aren't paying attention. Your job as a commanding officer is to make sure that the morale of your staff is in top shape."

"I thought it was in top shape."

Coollege turned her back, studied the tiny desk, and said, "Mine's at a low ebb right now."

Price held up his hands in mock surrender. He knew when he had been defeated. "Okay. Okay. You want to have dinner with me tonight."

"No, I don't think so. Not tonight." Then, grinning broadly, "Oh, if you insist."

"I don't remember insisting," said Price. "Not at all."

"You would have," said Coollege. "If I hadn't caved in so fast you would have insisted."

Price stretched and heard the quiet popping of his muscles as he did. He thought again about sleep but shook himself, driving the thought from his mind. He turned, grabbed his uniform jacket from the back of the chair, and said, "Well, let's get this show on the road. I want to get to bed."

"I don't believe I said anything about bed. I just wanted something to eat."

"Yes, ma'am," said Price with mock respect.

CHAPTER
5

Stone decided that he wanted to work with Lieutenant Eva Hamstein and Sergeant Thomas Wilcox. He knew them both well, had worked with them in the past, and trusted their instincts. They would be a good team for the mission at hand.

They were scheduled to meet in the conference room. Stone entered and found the other two there already. He sat down, looked at the pot, and asked, "That coffee?"

"As far as I know," said Hamstein. She was a young woman, tall but stocky. Her blond hair, when free, would hang to her shoulders. At the moment it was swept and pinned up. She had light brown eyes and a heavy jaw.

Stone pulled the pot toward him, lifted the top, and sniffed. "Yeah. It's coffee." He poured a cup and then said, "Eva, are you going to have a problem here?"

"Meaning what?"

"You outrank me but this is my mission. I call the shots on it."

"Oh, hell, Rocky, you should know better than that. Just

remember that I hold the rank and we'll get along. You want to take the responsibility, you go right ahead.''

"Tom, how about you?"

"We have the same rank," he said. Wilcox was also tall and stocky but had light hair and blue eyes. His hands were huge, looking as if they belonged on a man twice his size.

"Okay," said Stone. He sipped the coffee for a moment and then asked, "Anyone brief you about this?"

Hamstein shook her head. "We were just told to be here this morning and talk to you."

"This one should be volunteer," said Stone, "but I was told that I could have whoever I wanted."

"I'm not sure I like the sound of this," said Wilcox. "Not at all."

Stone drained his coffee and said, "We've been asked to grab a couple of people off Bolton's Planet and bring them back here for interrogation."

"That's all?" asked Wilcox. "That's an afternoon's worth of work."

"We're supposed to show a little finesse doing it," said Stone.

"Even so," said Hamstein, "it's not a major problem. Biggest problem is to have an escape route figured out before we make planetfall."

Stone stared at her. "You don't have a problem with this? You feel good about it?"

"What's the big deal?" asked Wilcox.

Stone turned his attention to Wilcox and then shrugged. "Okay. Let's get at it. I've drawn up a plan. I'll be dropping dirtside as part of the anthropological unit."

"I love it," said Hamstein.

Stone touched a button to bring up the display and said, "I'll run through this once. Take a look at it and then we'll critique the plan, making what modifications we need to pull it off."

"How soon do we drop dirtside?"

"Friday."

• • •

Price and Coollege spent their time in briefings organized by the anthropological unit. They listened to reports, read documents, and sat quietly with electrodes hooked to their heads as information was force-fed to them. They learned the history of Bolton's Planet, from the moment the explorer, in a ship that barely reached the system and then crash-landed on the largest of the continents, radioed his location to the colonialization of it. They learned of the first settlers who, wanting an idyllic settlement away from the problems of Earth, landed and established a strict society.

They sat back as they were taken on a holoed trip through the capital city, New Washington, where white stone had been used to construct a metropolis of beauty. It was almost like the domed cities on Earth where access was strictly controlled through computers and tourists lined up for months, waiting for a chance to visit. Governmental employees, as well as the leaders, walked to work, wore white robes, and acted out of a sense of duty, controlling every aspect of the lives of the people to eliminate waste, crime, need, and aggression.

They saw, using maps, how the infection had spread from the capital, outward across the continents until the whole planet was under the influence of the single government. Everything was strictly regulated, from the moment a person was born until they died.

After a couple of grueling days, Price pulled the electrodes from his head, draped them over the arm of the chair, and massaged his temples. "I just don't believe it," he said.

Coollege sat spent in her chair, sweat beading on her forehead and upper lip, and staining the collar of her uniform. "How can they live like that? Bees in a hive."

"Bees might have more freedom," said Price. "They can get out of the hive."

Coollege leaned forward, elbows on her knees, and stared down at the deck. "I wouldn't believe that people would subject themselves to something like that."

"You go with the flow," said Price. "You're born into the society and accept it until you have an opportunity, as an adult, to review the situation. That school. Students are taken in at age five. They live there, eat there, and are taught there. Everything strictly controlled by the state. They don't know that there is another way."

"Still, they have trouble."

"Sure. Mental disease and sociological behavior but they deal with those quickly and efficiently."

She took a deep breath and exhaled audibly. "I couldn't do it."

"If you were born to it . . ."

"That bit about sex. Through careful genetic engineering and advanced nutrition they have been able to increase the frequency of sex to two or three times a month. Where in the hell did they get that one?"

Price sat for a moment and then said, "Communal kitchens. Everyone eats the same foods and there is obviously something in it that dampens the sex drive."

"Don't you see?" asked Coollege, looking up at him. "That's the point. They've taken life and changed it from something that belongs to the individual to something that belongs to the state. That's not right."

"Ours is not to judge the society," said Price.

"Bull," said Coollege.

"It's not bull. We observe and report to headquarters but we don't pass on value judgments about that society."

"You must have feelings . . ."

"I said nothing about feelings," said Price. "I was commenting on what our job is. We're not supposed to let our personal emotions color our thinking."

Coollege thought about that and then said, "I think that was what I was trying to say."

"Then we are in agreement."

"I guess, Tree. I just don't like what I've seen down there."

"And I'm working on ignoring those feelings," said

Price. He turned toward the hatch but no one appeared. "I guess we're finished for the day. Let's walk by the office and see what the status of the mission is."

Coollege finished taking the electrodes from her head and dropped them into the seat of the chair. She ran her hands through her short hair, trying to straighten it.

Together they left the classroom and walked toward their office. The lights of the corridor were bright, indicating that it was still day duty hours. Few people were in the corridor. Most were at their stations or in their cubes. The command suggested that movement be restricted.

They found Stone in the office, sitting at the console, studying the center screen. It was a street scene on the planet's surface. Just a general scene with people strolling the walks looking as if they had no cares and no destination.

Price took the other chair and asked, "When do you make planetfall?"

"Tomorrow morning. I'm going down with the delegation but we've a fast ship that will be tagging along."

"You over the problem with the kidnapping, Rocky?" asked Coollege.

"Nope," Stone said. "But I can't see any way out of it without going down in flames myself."

"Tomorrow?" asked Price.

"First thing."

"There any other messages?"

"No, sir. I checked the board. Everything is clean for the moment."

"I guess that's it for the day," said Price. He looked at Coollege. "You interested in some dinner."

"Sure."

"Rocky?"

"No, thanks, Captain. I got a couple of last-minute things to catch up on and then I'm meeting with Eva and Tom for a great last feast."

Price shrugged. "How long for your mission?"

"Twenty-four hours . . . thirty-six at a max. Since we

don't have a specific target, just a source of data, almost anyone will do.''

Price, with Coollege, headed for the hatch. "I'll see you before you take off tomorrow.''

"Please do,'' said Stone, grinning broadly. "I'm going down as a full colonel.''

"Yes, sir,'' said Price. "We'll try.''

The landing team, including "Colonel" Stone, assembled in the ready room next to the main shuttle bay. They brought everything that would be needed dirtside and there were enlisted personnel gathering it, cataloging it, and preparing it for storage in the shuttle.

Stone sat with his feet up, grinning at some of the people who were staring at him. They were trying to figure out who the new colonel was, why they had heard nothing of his arrival on the ship, and why they hadn't been promoted themselves instead of him.

After twenty minutes, they were told they could board the shuttle. Stone entered the bay and noticed Hamstein and Wilcox, wearing flight gear, standing at one of the small interplanetary craft. It could hold as many as five or six depending on the size of the people and the cargo necessary. Hamstein straightened up and looked right at Stone. She didn't really smile but looked amused when she saw him. She didn't wave and bent back to her work.

Stone, using the tiny radio transmitter hidden in his button, said quietly, "Do you copy this?''

Now Wilcox looked up. He held a oil-blackened rag in one hand. He watched Stone for a moment as he wiped his hands on the rag.

"Guess you can hear me,'' said Stone.

Wilcox nodded slightly and then turned, saying something to Hamstein.

Stone turned his attention back to the landing team. Some of the lower-ranking members had already boarded. The command staff stood near the hatch, talking in quiet tones.

At the far end of the shuttle bay, behind the glass panel of the control room, a dozen technicians were working. Stone had expected someone from the colonel's staff to be there to see them off, but no one showed up.

The landing team leader finally said, "I think we'd better board now."

Just before he stepped up, into the shuttle, Stone took one final look around. He didn't see Price or Coollege, but wasn't concerned about that. Sometimes it was better if the military intelligence staff members slipped into the mission without being watched by the rest of the team, even though he'd wanted to flaunt his new rank. He'd show them when he reported back in a day or so.

"I guess this is it," said Stone, realizing that he was echoing the words that had probably been first spoken by the first humans to ever enter into a battle.

Stone climbed into the shuttle, started to drop into the closest seat, and then remembered he was a colonel. He could take almost any seat he wanted. That was going to be a decided advantage on the mission.

CHAPTER

6

The reception committee met them at the spaceport. Stone searched for signs of damage done during Price's escape, but if there was any, it had been repaired and covered so that it was impossible to spot.

He watched as the leader of the landing team, Colonel Richard White, met with the government representative, a small man, Brother Titus, wearing an off-white robe. Bright yellow trimmed it. His functionaries, both male and female, stood behind him, their robes the same color but the trim varied from green to blue to red. No one carried anything.

Stone listened to the people talk with half his mind. He was watching the activities in the terminal building. Passengers passed through control points where a computer checked with its massive memory to make sure that each person had an authorization to fly. One man was turned back, but rather than protest, he shrugged and left the line, walking toward the terminal exit. The people moved forward quietly, orderly, walking down the right side of the building and avoiding those who had exited flights that had landed earlier.

The man with the yellow piping waved a hand and everyone began to walk toward the front of the terminal. Other passengers got out of the way, bowing slightly.

"Everyone is so polite," said one of the women. "No one pushing."

"Pushing does no good," said Brother Titus. "Eventually we all reach our destination and if we move carefully, no one is injured."

"People always want to be first," said the cultural anthropologist, Sharon Hall. She wore a modified uniform but wasn't a line officer.

"People want what they have learned to want," said Brother Titus. "If they have been taught manners and consideration, and that being tenth in line is as good as being first, then stress in a society has been reduced."

"There are certain elements of human nature. These are bred into each of us. It is part of the genetic heritage of the human race," said Hall.

They reached the front of the terminal and a man in a green coverall ran forward to the open door. He stepped back, out of the way, his eyes downcast.

Brother Titus moved through and said, "Thank you, brother. Your kindness will be rewarded."

As they stepped into the bright light of the warm morning, a hover car slipped close to them and then settled to the ground. Brother Titus said, "I'm afraid that we all won't be able to travel in a single car."

White turned and said, "Let's break into two groups for the trip into the city. Colonel Stone, would you please take charge of the second group."

"Certainly, Colonel," said Stone. He knew what White was doing. Stone was, in effect, the lowest-ranking member of the team, but he was making it look as if he was one of the highest. White was setting it up so that Stone would be able to complete his mission easily.

"Sister Susan," said Brother Titus, "please accompany our guests so that we won't become separated."

"Our luggage?" asked Hall.

"Will be delivered to the hotel for you."

"Thank you," said White.

When the first car was loaded, the second slipped into place. Stone noticed that half the seats were occupied by men in white coveralls but all had red piping on them. All were big men, with dark hair chopped short. It looked like a security team to him, and Stone didn't like that.

"Colonel?" said Sister Susan.

"Please, let's have the rest board first. It was a cramped flight from our ship."

He delayed as long as he could, watching as the people circulated at the airport. It was an amazing contrast from what he had seen when they had obtained the cube and then had escaped from the planet. Everything was so calm, so low-key. The pace was slow, almost languid. No one rushed as if hurrying to catch a last-minute flight. No one pushed past those walking slower. The pace of everyone seemed to be the same.

Stone finally climbed into the hover car and it lifted, slipping along the designated route. He noticed that the pathway was divided into four lanes, two heading into the spaceport and two heading away. Between them was a large pedestrian area filled with walking people and bicycle riders. Everyone nodded or spoke to everyone else.

Stone twisted around and noticed that everyone had been paired with one of the locals. He could think of them only as security guards. The guards were watching very closely, which would make his job that much more difficult. But then a guard, geared to this society, might be an excellent source of information. Maybe his problem was solved. A security guard was not as innocent as the man or woman on the street.

Sister Susan began to speak as they cleared from the spaceport perimeter and headed into the city. Not a tall, narrow city from Earth, but a low, spread-out area, filled with grass-covered malls, three- and four-story buildings surrounded by trees, and a central area of shops, offices, and research centers. The "combat zone" was hidden from view, on the far side of New Washington.

As they worked their way into the center of the capital, Sister Susan said, "As you can see, we have removed, as much as possible, the causes of stress in our society. We believe that many of Earth's problems were caused by instant communications. If you can identify a problem immediately, then you require an immediate solution. If we can build a cushion into that exchange of information, we can remove some of the stress." She looked right at Stone and asked, "Don't you believe that to be so, Colonel?"

"I would think that delaying the communication and therefore the solution would create an even larger problem," said Stone carefully.

"But how important, really, are these problems. We learn that a shipment of, say, milk has gone to the wrong distribution center. An immediate phone call tells others of the problem and they feel obligated to run for the solution. But the question that must be asked is whether the misdelivery of milk is a large problem and can't it be solved in a more leisurely fashion without causing unneeded anxiety."

"That is certainly one way of viewing it," said Stone noncommittally.

The hover car rocked to a halt and Sister Susan, still standing, bent at the knees, looking out the window. "Ah, we've arrived already. A pleasant enough ride."

When the door opened, Stone stepped out and then walked toward the rear of the car. He watched the locals as they strolled through the city center. They had the same contented, no, blank look on their faces as those at the spaceport. They seemed to have something to do, some place to go, but they were in no hurry to get there.

"Inside, we'll have an opportunity to meet again with

Brother Titus, and the head of the government, Father Bob," said Sister Susan.

"Father Bob," said Stone.

"Yes. He believes that an informal policy is the best. We are, after all, part of a single family, striving to better ourselves and create a better world for our children."

Stone stood on the sidewalk and felt shivers run down his back. The sun was bright and hot overhead, but still he felt chilled. Everything looked calm and peaceful, but there was something frightening about this. When he'd been dirtside before, with Price and Coollege, they'd had a single, quick mission into a part of New Washington that remained hidden now. They'd been in one small part of the town without a chance to observe the society as a whole. They had not dealt with the society at large. All this was beginning to frighten him.

"Let's all go inside."

Again the door was opened by a man in a green coverall. He stepped out of their way as they passed by him. They walked across the marble floor and reached escalators that took them slowly to the next level. The interior was open and bright. Flags hung from poles angled toward the glassed ceiling over them, but they were flags that Stone didn't recognize. Through the glass overhead, he could see clouds building, sometimes hiding the sun for short periods, dimming the interior slightly.

There were people in colored coveralls moving around the building, nodding to one another, moving with a real sense of purpose. These were dedicated people, helping to benefit their fellow human beings.

Sister Susan held up a hand and gestured toward one of the side doors. "We'll find our friends in here."

The door opened onto a large room, softly carpeted and decorated in muted tones. A long table nearly bisected it and was piled with food and drink. White's team, along with locals in colored robes, were scattered around the table.

White sat in a high-backed chair, a plate of food in his

hand. "This stuff is delicious," he announced when he saw the others entering.

Stone walked across the room and stood at one of the floor-to-ceiling windows. It looked out on a green central plaza. Kids were playing a variety of games that involved running and jumping and a large red ball that looked as if it had been filled with helium.

Sister Susan pointed to the table and said, "I think our sessions will progress easier if we all have something to eat first. Please help yourselves."

Stone moved to the table without a word, built a sandwich, and poured a cup of juice. He found a place to sit and then watched the others as they went about their work. He ate his sandwich slowly as the planetary representatives circled, making sure that everyone in the landing team was happy. There was very little conversation.

When we finished with his plate, someone swooped down to take it so that he wouldn't be inconvenienced. Stone stood then and wondered how he could break away from the main team without raising suspicion. He wanted to get the mission started as quickly as possible and get the hell off the planet.

He started for the door and was intercepted by a tall woman with blond hair wearing a bright white robe trimmed in crimson. She took his arm and asked, "Is there something that you need, brother?"

Stone grinned sheepishly and said, "Latrine . . . ah, the rest room."

"Oh. Please come with me."

Stone reluctantly followed her to a short hallway and was directed into the rest room. He found a stall and entered, sitting as he pondered his next move. Under normal circumstances he would have just gone out for a walk but this society was more controlled and it was obvious they weren't going to let him out of his own. Someone would be with him as he made every move. They were watching all those on the landing team very closely.

When he returned to the main room, a screen had been lowered at one end, the windows had been covered, dimming the area significantly. The chairs had been arranged so that everyone was sitting facing the main screen. The food-laden tables had disappeared.

Brother Titus stood near the screen and said, "We have prepared a short documentary, letting you see how we have solved many of the problems that have plagued the human race from the beginning of time. We're hoping to take our solutions off-world soon and allow the rest of the galaxy to share in the secret of our peace."

Stone took a chair at the rear of the room and thought there was nothing worse than people who believed they had all the answers for humanity's problems because they began trying to force those answers on those who didn't want them. He sat quietly but didn't watch the film.

When it ended, to trumpet fanfares and glowing scenes of a sunset on Bolton's Planet, Brother Titus said, "I know that you all have many questions, but those must wait. We'll escort you to your quarters now so that you may settle in. Relax for the afternoon. We have planned for an instructional program tonight. An introduction to our society."

With that the lights came up and the blinds were pulled from the windows. The locals, in their long robes, moved among the members of the landing team. Each person had an escort, and together, they were led from the room, out into the center area. They were split into smaller groups, led down a long, wide, bright corridor. There were people circulating through the area, all moving with the same contented pace.

Hall said, "Everyone looks so happy here."

"They are," said Brother Titus. "Full employment. No one has a want or a need. Universal health care. No hunger. No homeless."

"But at what cost?" asked White.

Brother Titus slowed and turned. "There are some restrictions on individual freedoms, but these are trival concerns, freedoms that mean little to society. We have found our solution.''

They left the building, walking down a short flight of steps and across a large central plaza. It was grass-covered and tree-lined, looking as peaceful as a country meadow. A few children were running toward another building, laughing as they disappeared.

''Returning to class,'' said Brother Titus, nodding toward the children. ''Universal education through our system is geared to selecting the occupation best suited to the ability and talents of the individual. Rather than letting everyone try to be a pilot or a video star, we determine the best job for the person and then gently push him or her toward that occupation. We have no vacant jobs in''—he grinned—''garbage collection. There are those who are best suited for that.''

Stone was beginning to form a picture of the planet that was distinctly different from the one he'd had before landing. Somehow the information had been skewed so that the rigidity of the society hadn't been obvious. Of course, seeing the ''combat zone'' had provided a picture of a planet that was not quite as structured as the one he was now seeing.

They entered another building, again with a large atrium that rose to the top with rows of rooms around the exterior. ''This is our finest hotel,'' said Brother Titus, waving a hand to encompass the interior. ''You'll be quite comfortable while you stay with us.''

They bypassed the registration desk and were escorted directly to their rooms, each person with one of the planet's representatives. The blonde stuck with Stone, opening the door for him and then showing the comforts of the room.

''Planetwide television here,'' she said, opening the console. ''I'm afraid that most of our fare is educational in nature. Television has a real power to educate when it is used properly.''

''Entertainment?'' asked Stone.

"Some programming later in the evening before sign-off at midnight."

Stone looked at the room carefully. There was a king-size bed that looked luxurious after the cramped cube on the ship. It had a private bath complete with a shower and a tub, a large sitting area with chairs and a table, and a balcony that overlooked the heart of the city. The room was decorated in light, airy colors that ran to reds, yellows, and orange. Stone wondered if it would be possible to sleep in that environment. The colors seemed to scream at him.

The blonde bowed slightly at the waist and said, "If there is anything you need, I will be more than happy to serve."

For a moment Stone thought of asking her if that included sharing his bed and then decided against it. He was afraid the answer would be "Yes."

After showing him the workings of the room, all the conveniences built into it, the controls for the climate control and lights, she left, saying that she would be close if he needed anything. "This button," she said, stroking it with her thumb, "will summon me. Please use it."

"Thank you," said Stone. When she was gone, he walked to the balcony and looked at the city. He realized that she had never told him her name. And then he realized that things just were not what they seemed.

CHAPTER

7

Price was sitting in the intelligence office watching the progress of the men and women of the landing team on Bolton's Planet. The landing team couldn't broadcast from the planet's surface without revealing that they were in contact with the ship, but Price could monitor them as they landed and then entered the city. When the terrain was clear and open, they could keep the landing team under surveillance.

But as soon as they entered the city, they were lost in the clutter there. Price tried to fine-tune the computer, but there were too many humans in New Washington. A very skilled technician might be able to detect the landing team, but he couldn't do it. Instead, he turned off the computer and looked over at Coollege. "I guess, that's it."

"Now what?"

"Well, I think we're through for the day. Nothing more to do until Stone returns with the prisoners."

"Then we can go to the lounge to relax," she said.

Grinning, Price said, "If that's what you want. I'd thought about something a little more private."

"You're getting awful sure of yourself lately, Tree. I'm not sure that I like that."

"Then let's go to the lounge. I was just thinking that we're easy to find there. Out in the open where the colonel could spot us, and I'm not sure that I want to be in easy range. If they see you taking it easy, they feel obligated to find you something constructive to do."

"Afraid that something's going to happen?" she asked.

"No, Jackknife, I'm not afraid that anything will happen. What could happen?"

"Stone gets thrown into jail because they recognize him as the man who took the cube from you."

"Even if they could, with him a member of a diplomatic mission to the planet's surface, they're not going to arrest him. Not now anyway."

"Don't be so sure. Those guys aren't playing by the same rules as the rest of us."

Price turned and touched one of the computer keyboards and then stopped. "I was going to show you the aggressiveness profile on those people, as determined by the Laidlaw complex, but what's the use?"

Now she laughed. "I can't believe that you'd ever look at something like that. Our own experiences show that it is irrelevant. They chased us off the planet's surface with lasers blazing. Someone down there is aggressive and not afraid to shoot at people."

"True," said Price, standing and stretching. "Anyway, let's get out of here. And there is one thing that I've been meaning to ask you."

"What's that?"

"I'm called Tree for obvious reasons . . . Joshua Tree, and Stone is called Rocky, but why are you called Jackknife? That just doesn't seem to fit."

"Is this relevant?"

They moved to the hatch and it irised opened. Once they

had stepped through, Price locked the office. As they walked down the corridor, he said, "Not relevant at all."

"It was something that came about in training. I was dumped on an isolated planet . . . you know the drill. It's designed to see how well you think in a hostile environment with nothing but the clothes on your back."

"Right." Price remembered that he'd lasted nearly two hours before the locals had him cornered in a decaying old barn with authorities swooping down from above. It hadn't been a glowing moment in his training. He'd been found by the locals almost immediately.

"When they dropped us, I managed to sneak a jackknife down with me. I didn't know what good it would do to have it, but I just wanted a weapon. No one else had been able, or had even thought about it."

"So what did you do with it?" asked Price.

"That's the thing. It was just about useless to me. We were set down on the outskirts of an old city and told to survive until the pickup ship came. Half the people were arrested in the first hour or so. I managed to slip away, found some old clothes, and stole them. I walked into town, swiped a purse, and checked into a ratty hotel using the ID card and cash I had stolen. I slept with the knife under the pillow but didn't need it. When I wanted something, I slipped out at night, and when the time was up, I just left the hotel. I walked to the pickup point. Nothing to it."

"So why do they call you Jackknife?"

"Because I still had that at pickup. They couldn't believe I'd managed to sneak it down."

They reached the lounge. Coollege sat down looking out at the starfields and Price found them something to drink. He handed her a glass and then sat, propping his feet in one of the other chairs.

"This is the worst," he said. "The waiting. Can't do anything until Stone makes his move. Can't help him and can't give him orders. Just wait for him to succeed or to screw up."

She sipped at the beverage. "But it is better being here, waiting, than it is being down there. No danger to us."

"I don't think so. Down there I would know what is happening. I'd be in charge. Here, there is nothing that can be done. And if he screws up, then the colonel is going to blame me. That makes me nervous."

Coollege put her glass to one side and then leaned over, taking Price's hand in hers. She turned and looked up into his eyes. "Waiting's the only thing we can do now."

"Not the only thing," said Price. "Just one of the things."

Hamstein and Wilcox had followed the larger ship, hiding in its radar shadow. They had stayed close until they approached near to Bolton's Planet and then let their ship slip back until they entered a parking orbit forty thousand miles above New Washington. With their instruments, their sensors, their equipment, they could see down into the city. If they used everything, they would begin to radiate electromagnetic signals that could be detected, so they were content to sit forty thousand miles up and watch the points of light below them. Their radar signal was small and their EM signature was nearly nonexistent at the moment.

Hamstein had locked the orbit in, letting the computer fly the scout ship, and then had left the cockpit area. If anything came close, if they were scanned, if their trajectory or heading or altitude shifted slightly, a warning bell would sound to alert her. She would have more than enough time to return and correct the problem if the navigational and flight computers were unable to fix it without her help.

Wilcox had been sitting in the passenger area, his feet up, reading a hand-held book. When he began to drift off, feeling sleepy, he pulled the cassette from the reader and set it aside. He stretched out, his eyes closed as he listened to the rumble of the engine and the whine of the small servos and motors on the ship.

Hamstein sat down on the deck near him, reached up, and

began to rub his shoulders. When he opened his eyes, she said, "We're in orbit now. Landing team is down and safe for the moment."

Wilcox rolled to his side, hiked his knees up, and cradled his head on his arm. He reached over to squeeze her shoulder. "Alone again. Funny how this keeps working out. You think that Rocky knows?"

She smiled and shook her head. "Nah. He's just picking the people he knows best and trusts the most. He knows we won't let him down."

Wilcox lifted a hand and rubbed his eye. "I suppose it's going to be a while before anything happens down there."

"Rocky will have to separate himself from the main team and locate the victims. I think we've probably several hours before we need to make the pickup what with welcoming speeches and all that."

"Things could get boring real fast," said Wilcox.

"That's the thing on these little scout ships," said Hamstein, "nothing much to do. Just sit around and stare at the instruments that we have to keep turned off so that we don't leave an electromagnetic signature."

"I can think of something," said Wilcox. He shifted around and reached for the Velcro on Hamstein's flight suit. He slipped a finger in and pulled it down with a loud ripping sound.

"I don't think you're supposed to be doing that," Hamstein said. "I'm an officer and you're only an NCO."

"Want me to stop?"

"I was just commenting on what the regulations say. Besides, one of us should be on watch."

Wilcox rolled to his back and stared at the overhead. "If you were concerned about watch, why did you come back here?"

"To see if I could get you in some kind of an uproar. Looks like I succeeded."

Wilcox grinned and reached around, pulling her close. As she twisted to face him, Wilcox slipped his fingers into the front of her flight suit. He noticed that she was wearing some kind of light T-shirt.

"What in the hell?"

"I didn't know that you were going to be amorous," she said.

"And I thought you were going to stay in the cockpit watching the little lights flash."

She shrugged her shoulders and pulled the top of the flight suit away. "How's that?"

Wilcox got up and then sat down on the deck facing her, his legs folded under him. He slipped his hands under the fabric of her shirt and rubbed her ribs. She leaned forward, closer to him.

"This is the way we should spend more time," she said, her voice husky.

"It's up to you."

She rocked back and grabbed the tails of her shirt, lifting it up, over her head. She tossed it to the side, away from them completely.

At that moment one of the buzzers went off. A quiet chirp that alerted them to a problem.

Hamstein stood up, laughing. "Now isn't that always the way." She didn't bother to retrieve her T-shirt, but pulled the top of her flight suit up, over her shoulders. She ignored the Velcro as she worked her way back to the cockpit.

Wilcox was right behind her. He looked over her shoulder. "What's going on?"

"We've been detected. Sensor sweeps from the planet's surface. Looks like they're holding on us."

"So what do we do?"

"We can move out of this orbit, taking the ship higher, divert toward their moon and use it to mask, or stay right here. We are, basically, in free space."

Wilcox slipped into the other seat and looked at the instruments arrayed around them. He watched as one of the screens crawled with numbers and words as the diagnostic system checked the various components of the controls.

"They're watching us pretty close now that they've found us," said Hamstein.

"Then let's get out."

"We move too far and Rocky's going to have trouble getting us and it'll increase our response time."

"They know we're here," said Wilcox, "and that can't be very good."

"No," said Hamstein, agreeing. She reached forward and touched a switch but didn't flip it. Instead she turned her attention to the screen. "I think they're tracking us with the planetary defense. We're burned."

"Rocky will have to get along without us," said Wilcox. "For a few minutes anyway."

Hamstein nodded and said, "I'm going to break us out of orbit then. We'll climb toward their moon, use it to mask, and hang there."

"Go."

Hamstein shifted around in her seat and then buckled her seat belt and shoulder harness. She reached out, touched the controls, and put her feet on the controls. "Are you ready to break orbit?"

Wilcox had followed suit. He was strapped in, head back against the rest. "Ready."

Hamstein set the controls and said, "Thirty seconds to booster burn."

Wilcox sat quietly and studied the control panel. He checked out the VDT, showing the planet under them. He watched the sensors, showing the planet's equipment focused on them. He glanced at the radar and saw there was nothing close to them.

"Running might not be the right thing," he said.

"We're committed now."

"Might tell them that we're afraid of them."

She ignored the comment. "Here we go." She pushed the throttle forward. There was an increase in the rumble behind them and both were pushed gently back into their seats. "Orbit has been broken."

Wilcox watched as New Washington dwindled on the screen. He could have increased the magnification but didn't bother. Instead he switched the view to the tiny moon. He studied it but saw nothing there of interest. No sign of a planetary outpost. No sign of a remote-control observation base.

"We're at forty-two thousand miles and increasing the altitude," she said.

"Sensor problems seemed to have stopped," said Wilcox.

"Lost their focus on us," said Hamstein.

"You going to break off the climb-out now?"

"Let's just keep moving for a while. If we drop right back, they'll probably find us again. That'll raise their suspicions about us even more."

"Nothing they can do about it," said Wilcox.

Hamstein relaxed and pulled back on the control. "We're about to enter orbit around their moon."

"How long are we going to sit here?"

"A couple of hours. Then we'll drop back where we're supposed to be."

"Ready for Rocky."

"If he needs us."

CHAPTER

8

Stone believed that it would be easiest to slip away at night. Darkness covered a variety of sins and he was going to use it to his advantage. There might be fewer people about, but there would be some, and the night would be his ally.

He spent some time sitting on the edge of the bed, flipping among the three television channels, but the programming all had a sameness to it. In-depth looks at manufacturing centers, documentaries on the heroes who had settled the planet, reports on the improvements made to life on the planet, and a few short segments highlighting the accomplishments of the government and its leaders. Stone had never seen anything more boring. As a school kid he had looked forward to such documentaries, but as an adult with no alternatives, he recognized them for what they were. Poorly created propaganda and nothing more.

When his escort called to ask when she should pick him up for the evening activities, Stone had begged off, saying that he was slightly ill. He claimed it was the result of the spaceflight and then excitement of being on a new planet.

"I could bring you something to eat," she volunteered.

"No, that's not necessary. Please, just forget about me," said Stone. "I'll be fine if I can catch a little sleep. That's all I need."

"I can check on you in an hour or so."

"No. Please, don't put yourself out. I think I'll just lay down and take a nap," said Stone. "I just need some sleep and then I'll be fine."

The woman was quiet for a moment and then said, "If you need anything, please give me a call. I'm here to serve you."

"Sure."

When she signed off, Stone went into the bathroom and took a quick shower. A robe, like those worn by most of the leaders, was hanging on the back of the door. He donned it and then walked back into the main room, examining himself in the mirror. He thought he looked as if he belonged on the planet, but he couldn't be sure. Sometimes there were subtle things that needed to be done. Little things that everyone who lived there understood, even if they hadn't been explained, but that outsiders might not notice. It was a way of buttoning the garment, or of standing. It was often the little things that gave away the impostor.

On old Earth, he remembered reading an account of Allied soldiers who had escaped from a Nazi prisoner of war camp and were waiting at a railroad station, hoping to catch a train out. One of the Americans was spotted by the way he held his cigarette. The Americans held it between two fingers while Germans often cupped it in the palm, almost as if shielding the tip from the weather.

Little things could give him away, but there was no time to worry about that. He needed to get out, into society, and complete his mission. And one of the reasons for the mission was so that the next team, whose job was more difficult, would be aware of those little things. Stone only had to pass for an hour or two. They would have to pass for days on end, never giving a hint that they didn't belong.

Stone walked back to his balcony and sat down to watch the sunset. The people, finished with the day's labors, were now returning to their residences. Children ran through the parks laughing out loud. Parents stood or sat on the side, watching as the children had their fun. It was a laid-back scene with no hint of aggression or pressure to perform. Not like on Earth where parents would be telling their children to win, to compete, to outwit the others.

As the sun faded, concealed lights began to brighten. Lights hidden by the trees, on the sides of the buildings, in the walkways, making the world nearly as bright at night as it was in the day. Darkness came slowly, but it was pushed back by civilization.

Stone looked at his watch. The reception would be in full swing and those there would be occupied. They would have no time to think about the anthropologist who was sick and unable to attend. No one would be calling on him for several hours. It was time to begin his search.

He pushed himself from the chair and walked across the room. He opened the door and stepped into the hallway. He turned and walked toward the escalators and took one down to the lobby. There he found a number of people, most of them locals, dressed in robes or coveralls, talking quietly in groups. There was nothing to set them apart from any other group he had seen since arriving.

The door to the outside was always open, a column of air blowing from top to bottom, designed to keep insects and bad weather out but to allow people to walk through easily. As he stepped into the warm evening, he wondered about insects. He'd seen none, though he hadn't looked all that hard. But what did it say about a society that would eliminate the insects, or force them to such a low level of population that they were next to invisible?

He turned and began to walk quickly toward the residential complexes. As he reached a corner, he nearly collided with a man who held up both hands, almost as if to show he held no weapon, and said, "Slow down, brother. What's your hurry?"

"Of course, brother," said Stone, smiling. "I wasn't paying attention."

He then continued on, walking slowly, as if on a stroll, nodding to the people he passed. He reached the park and sat down on a bench with a young couple who was holding hands and who had no time for anyone else.

A child ran up, stopped directly in front of him, handed him a flower, and then whirled, running away. There was something to be said for a world where the youngsters could approach a stranger with no fear at all.

Again Stone was struck by the absence of insects. And the absence of animals. There was nothing in the park that didn't belong there. Beautiful plantings, shrubs, and bushes, but no rabbits or squirrels. It was an antiseptic world, clean to the point of being sterile.

A quiet bell sounded and when it did, the people began to head toward one of the many residence halls. No one lingered behind. Each person stopped what he or she was doing and headed home. Stone was amazed by the obedience that had been conditioned into each of the people. Even the soldiers he knew weren't that highly disciplined.

He stood up, and decided that the young couple would be the perfect targets. A man and a woman who were close enough to childhood to remember it clearly, yet adults who would be able to explain the differences and subtleties of the culture to the interrogators.

He followed them as they walked along a flagstone path lined with brightly colored flowers. Although he stayed close, they didn't seem suspicious of him, more interested in each other than in him.

They walked to one of the residence halls and entered through the front door. The lobby looked like the one in the hotel and included a large reception area filled with people sitting together and talking quietly.

The couple headed straight to the escalator and rode up to

the third floor. Stone was right behind them, watching every move they made and those of the people around them. They passed a television lounge where some kind of program was ending. The people began to filter out, but the corridor didn't seem crowded the way it would be back on Earth. Maybe it was because of the slow pace or the politeness of the people. They just walked toward their rooms, chatting with each other, paying almost no attention to what was going on around them.

A door opened and Stone caught a glimpse of the interior. No window on the far wall. A cot with a blanket looking more like a barracks than a room. A wall locker, small desk, and straight-backed chair. The same gray carpet was on the floor in the room as that in the corridor. It was designed for heavy wear and not for beauty.

"Are you lost, brother?" asked a woman.

Stone turned. The brunette had a towel wrapped around her waist and her hair was wet. She had apparently just come from the shower.

"I was just transferred here this morning. I'm afraid that I'm a little confused."

"There is an empty room at the end of the hall. On the right."

"Ah."

"You sound funny," she said, cocking her head to one side.

Stone smiled and said, "So do you."

"Welcome anyway, brother," she said. She turned and walked down the hall.

Stone watched her go, thinking how natural she had acted, as if she had been fully clothed. She didn't worry that he might be seeing something that he shouldn't. It was a refreshing attitude to see.

He walked to the end of the hall and opened the door. As he stepped in, the lights came on showing that the room, though furnished, was not occupied. The mattress of the cot had been rolled up and the bedding was stacked on it. The doors of the locker were open, showing that nothing was stored inside. The room was ready for its next occupant.

There was a tap at the door and Stone turned. A man, totally naked, stood there. "Hi," he said.

"Hi."

"Name's Joseph two two one."

Stone didn't move but said, "No Brother Joseph?"

"We're a little more informal here," said Joseph. "Welcome to the house."

"Thank you . . . brother."

"Do you need anything for the night? Toothpaste? Soap? You have everything?"

"Yes, thank you."

"Where's your kit?"

"Kit?"

"Spare clothes, hygiene gear, and the like."

"Coming up in a minute. I left it below until I found a place to stay."

"Oh." Brother Joseph turned and then stopped. "Anyway, welcome to the house."

"Thank you."

When Brother Joseph was gone, Stone closed the door and activated his tiny transmitter. "Swoop Two, this is Swoop One, are you there?"

A moment later a tinny voice filled with static said, "Standing by."

That was all he needed to hear. The odds of anyone locating him by the short transmission, or even hearing it without knowing about him already, was remote. Short and sweet and no one the wiser.

He walked to the cot and sat down on the edge of it. After several minutes, the light went out. There was no warning and that surprised him, causing him to stand. As he did, it came on again. Obviously it was geared to his motion, lighting when the occupant moved around signaling a need for light. That was interesting.

When the light went out again, he sat in the darkness,

listening to the sounds of the residence hall. People were talking and joking, but it was more subdued than anything he had heard before. Even on the ships, where rank was important and sergeants could keep the other enlisted men and women from having fun, there was more noise, more horseplay.

The noise level fell off rapidly and when Stone moved again, the light didn't come back on brightly. It was a dull red glow giving him enough light to see but not enough that would disturb anyone else. It seemed that it was now time for lights out.

"Interesting," he said again.

Now he moved back to the door and opened it. Lighting in the hallway was subdued, a dim red. No one was moving anywhere. No one was talking. Lights were out and everyone seemed to be in bed asleep. Stone wished that they could get the soldiers on the ships to respond that quickly to lights out.

Stone moved down the hallway to the communal bathroom and looked inside. The lights there were brighter than those in the hall but not much. He entered and walked to one of the mirrors to inspect himself. He knew that he was delaying the beginning of the mission because he just didn't want to do it. He'd rather pull out and head back to the ship. Get out while the getting was good.

The plan sprung into his mind full-blown. These people had no resistance to authority. It was obvious in the passive way they reacted to everything. A bell sounds and they all retreat to their rooms. It's announced that lights are out and they all go to bed. No complaint. No whining. They do as they are told. Therefore, a man appearing in the night, speaking with authority, could order them to do about anything. They wouldn't question him, assuming that the man was just who he claimed to be and had the authority to give the orders he was giving. A simple way to get them to follow him out was to order them to do so. He could then get them out where Hamstein and Wilcox could land. In minutes they would be heading for the main ship.

Stone walked down the hall and pushed on the closest door. He decided that he didn't have to find the young couple. Anyone would do. The door swung open, slowly revealing a single person sleeping on a cot. Stone stepped into the room and said, "You have to get up now."

The form didn't move at first, and Stone spoke louder, with more authority in his voice. "You must get up now."

The form stirred, rolled to its back, and raised hands over the head, stretching. She sat up, letting the sheet drop away. "What is it, brother?"

"It is required that you come with me now."

She swung her legs off the cot and sat up. "Of course. Let me grab a coverall."

"Please hurry," said Stone. He felt guilty staring at her, but didn't shift his eyes. Men had been killed because they didn't want a prisoner to experience a few moments of embarrassment.

She grabbed the coveralls and stepped into them, closing them as she slipped her feet into sandals. "Will we be gone for very long?"

"No. Please be quiet now." Stone turned, but before he entered the corridor added, "Others are asleep. We don't want to wake them."

"Of course."

They moved to the next door and Stone told the woman to wait. He stepped into the room, saw another female, and retreated. In the next room, he woke the occupant, a lone male. He gave the man the same orders and the man obeyed him with the same quickness.

Back in the hallway, the woman asked, "Where are we going to go now?"

"Out," said Stone. "A special assignment."

"Doesn't sound quite right to me," said the man.

"Brother," said the woman, "maybe we should check with our supervisors. This isn't right."

"It's been squared with them."

"Squared, brother?"

"Approved," said Stone quickly, thinking that he would have to be more careful.

"I don't recognize you, brother. What is the purpose of this trip?"

"Routine," said Stone, feeling it slip away from him. They were suspicious now and asking too many questions. He had to get them out of the building.

"Let's go," he said authoritatively. "Stay close and remain quiet. We don't want to wake the others."

"I want to check with Bob," said the man. "Only take a moment."

"I said, 'Let's go.'"

"Just wait," said the woman calmly.

"Just go down to the lobby," said Stone.

"Lobby? Oh, you mean the central rec. No, I want to talk to Bob first."

"No need for that. Let's move." Stone pushed the man toward the escalator and said, "Do it and you won't get hurt."

The man took two stumbling steps and then whirled. Stone expected him to raise his hands to fight, but instead he yelled, "Sick man out here. We have a sick brother."

That was the last thing that Stone had expected. A fight, a scream, but not a warning that there was a sick brother in the hallway.

Doors all along the corridor began to open. People stumbled out, some rubbing their eyes, most of them naked. Stone watched them for a moment and then said, "Fine. I'll take care of it by myself." All he could do was to just try to get away. The game was lost.

But the man wasn't going to allow that. He leapt forward and wrapped his arms around Stone, holding him in a bear hug. He continued to shout. "Sick man. Help us."

Others started forward, looking as if they wanted to help. Fright flickered in the eyes of some, but they came on anyway. If one of their brothers needed help, they were going to see that he got it.

Stone tried to break the grip of the man holding him, but he was stronger than he looked. Instead he stomped on the exposed toes, smashing them into the floor. The man roared in sudden pain and loosened his grip. Stone broke the man's grip and then punched the man once in the face, driving him back. He hit the wall and fell to the floor, blood pouring from his flattened nose. He held his hand up, trying to stop the blood, forgetting all about Stone.

Stone spun to run, but the woman stuck her foot out, tripping him. Stone sprawled to his hands and knees and the woman reached for his shoulder, saying over and over, "I'm sorry, brother. We must help you."

As he climbed to his feet, Stone shoved her away and she fell on the floor. He whirled, faced the oncoming people, and growled at them. That stopped them for a moment. He spun again and ran for the escalators that would get him out of the building.

He reached them and ran down the closest. He could hear shouting behind him but didn't care. Shouting behind him meant they were still trying to organize some kind of pursuit. They didn't know what to do.

As he reached the first level, a siren went off and the entire building brightened suddenly. A moment later a speaker announced, "We have a sick man in our building. Let's find him and help him. Everyone. Let's help him." The announcement repeated over and over.

Stone leapt from the escalator and ran around the end of it, taking it down to the main level. He ducked slightly, looking down, and saw the black-uniformed police pouring through the front doors. A dozen of them in riot gear, body armor, and carrying weapons. There was no way for him to fight through them. Not without a weapon of his own.

Touching the switch of his radio, he said, "Swoop One is in trouble. Locate."

"Two monitors."

Stone turned again and started back up the escalator. The brothers and sisters from above were coming at him, trying to force him into the cordon being created by the police. But Stone knew he would have a better chance against the untrained civilians above him. He charged into the crowd and knocked one man over rail. He fell onto the up escalator, his head hitting with the sound of a ripe melon.

"Grab him."

"Help him."

"I've got him now. Help me."

Stone punched the man in the face and he fell back, knocking two people down. Stone hurtled the three bodies and ran down a corridor. The people jumped out of his way. One man fell trying to get back into his room.

"There he goes. Down there."

"Someone grab him."

"He needs help. Help him."

Stone reached the end of the hall and tore open the door. He ran through it and started down the steps there. He hit the button on the transmitter. "Swoop One is in great trouble."

"Squawk ident."

Stone stopped on the landing, touched a microswitch, knowing that anyone could now home in on him, if they could find the signal. But it would tell Hamstein and Wilcox exactly where he was so they could get in to help him.

"We have you. You have to get clear of the building."

"I'm working on it. Timing is going to be critical."

"Roger that."

Stone reached the ground floor and pulled open the door and knew that it was all over. A ring of black-clad police, lights set up right behind them and a helicopter hovering overhead, were waiting for him. For a moment he thought about attacking them and then knew that it was no use. There were too many of them and they were all armed. He would never be able to burst through them.

Stone straightened up and raised his hands slowly,

grinning at them. He said, "I'm Colonel Wallace Stone and I'm with the landing team visiting here."

One of the black-clad men walked forward with a pistol in his hand. "I don't believe that we care who you are or who you're with. You're coming with us now."

"Certainly, sir," said Stone.

CHAPTER

9

White, along with Father Bob, Brother Titus, Sister Susan, and three of his senior officers, sat at the head table. They were served by youngsters dressed in brightly colored short tunics. They were ready with food or drink or clean silverware, though the silverware was gold-plated, as soon as it was needed by any of the guests.

The abundance of food was impressive, as was the size of the hall. For men and women who had been locked up in a spaceship for more than a year where ever square inch of space was strictly controlled and used, it was impressive to see high ceilings in a room that wasted so much space. There were huge areas designed simply to exist and for no other reason.

White was feeling good. He had sampled everything that had been set in front of him including half a dozen glasses of wine, beer, and liquor. He had stuffed himself with the exotic dishes until he had to unbutton the top of his pants and loosen his belt. He had laughed until his sides hurt and smiled until his face was sore. He was doing his best to make his hosts happy, proving that men and women of Earth were tolerant of all life-styles. He was taking his role as ambassador and diplomat as seriously as he took any of his jobs.

Brother Titus, who was keeping up with White, eating as much and drinking as much but who didn't laugh at all, had been studying the whole group as the evening progressed. Finally he leaned close to White and said, "I see that one of your staff is absent."

"Colonel Stone," said White. "I'm afraid that he was under the weather. Feeling poorly."

"I could have one of our doctors look in on him," said Brother Titus.

"No, I don't believe that it is anything that serious. A little rest will take care of it. He said that he was going to remain in his room to nap."

"If you're sure the doctor wouldn't be of benefit."

"Thank you for asking," said White, "but I believe it is unnecessary."

When they finished the food, Brother Titus stood, glanced down at the sleeping Father Bob, and clapped his hands together almost like a potentate on Earth two thousand years ago. All the doors flew open and boys and girls carrying banners and short poles with long ribbons ran into the ballroom. They danced to music that came from two dozen hidden speakers, finally stopping in two long, straight lines in front of the visitors.

"Some of our young people," said Brother Titus. "Listen to them."

Together the boys and girls praised their schools, their teachers, their leaders, and finally their planet. They snapped out the words together, so well rehearsed that it sounded like a single voice. They then sang a short song and danced out of the room.

"Very nice," said White when the last of the children had disappeared. "Very nice, indeed."

Brother Titus took a drink of wine and set his goblet on

the table. Again he glanced at the sleeping form of Father Bob. Then staring at White, he said, "Now, Colonel White, maybe you can explain exactly what you hope to learn here."

White looked at Titus and raised an eyebrow. "I'm afraid that I don't understand the question."

"It is kind of you to visit us but we are an independent planet. We have no need for assistance from you or anyone else. We are completely self-sufficient. Since we have requested no aid of any kind, I was merely asking why you have decided, at this time, to visit us."

"Of course," said White, nodding. "I understand all that. However, you are human, as are we, and we must all cooperate."

"Why?" asked Titus.

"Because we are all human. Those who are able help those who are not."

"I do not need a lecture on the human condition," said Titus evenly. "However, we provide our people with everything they need. We have everything that we need right here. We have no desire for outside contact."

"We are not interested in forcing ourselves on you," said White. "But we would like to open diplomatic channels for communications. I'm sure that we can help each other. No matter how self-sufficient one is, there are always things that one cannot provide for oneself."

A man in an off-white robe with red piping approached the table and leaned close to Titus. He whispered to him and then straightened, moving back away.

"It seems that your man, your Colonel Stone, wasn't as ill as you might have believed."

"I'm afraid that I don't understand."

"He broke into a residence hall, injured a number of our brothers and sisters, and had to be arrested. He is in custody now."

"I'm sure that you're aware that Colonel Stone enjoys diplomatic immunity."

"Ah," said Brother Titus. "No question about what he did, or his reasons for doing it, only that he enjoys diplomatic immunity. No, I'm afraid that a violation of our laws is not excused by agreements that were never endorsed by us. Colonel Stone will be examined by us and we will determine if he must stand trial for his actions tonight or if he will merely be expelled."

"I must protest most strongly," said White.

"And I must protest the illegal actions of your staff," said Titus. "He lied to us, violated our hospitality and laws, and has injured several of our citizens. Now, if you'll excuse me, I have other business to attend to. Sister Susan will guide you through the rest of the evening."

White stood up and wanted to protest further but knew it would do no good. The best course was to remain quiet and see what could be done behind the scenes.

Father Bob slumbered on, unaware of the trouble that was brewing.

Hamstein had dropped from the orbit near the moon and slipped closer to the planet, diving into the atmosphere and hanging only five hundred thousand feet above New Washington. She had turned off every piece of equipment that could generate an electromagnetic field and be detected, had ignored the navigation lights that could be seen, and had cut the engine power and masked the exhaust. The signature of her craft was reduced to the nearly invisible for the moment.

Wilcox sat at the navigator's station, watching the computer attempt to match the terrain far below them with the models that had been created for the stealth approach. With only passive sightings, the computer had created a three-dimensional picture on the screen.

"We're holding over the capital now. No indications of scanning by them. Looks like the city is shutting down for the night."

"You have Rocky located?"

"Got a good read on his signal at the moment. It's fairly

stationary. But if he keeps broadcasting, they're going to nail him.''

Hamstein took a deep breath and exhaled audibly. "At the moment, I don't think that is a major concern by him. Okay. We're set. Now it's up to him.''

Wilcox reached over and turned down the interior lights. He then watched the screen in front of him, looking like a display of a video game. It had plotted all aircraft—commercial, private, and military. Moving vehicles of a certain size or weight, trucks, tanks, armored cars, were also shown. Any military or police installations that had been identified were brightly illuminated. It gave him an idea of what was happening on the surface.

"Got some air activity near where Rocky is," said Wilcox. "Nothing extraordinary at the moment.''

"I wish we could see what was happening down there," said Hamstein. "This is getting hairy.''

"I could activate the rear camera.''

"No. That'll light up their detection board like a Christmas tree. That's not a passive system. Let's just be patient.''

"Sure.''

Wilcox kept his eyes on the screens, shifting from one to the next. He watched as the signal from Stone moved slightly and then began to fade.

"We're losing him.''

Hamstein leaned over and looked at the display. "Try to enhance.''

"It's at his end. There's not much I can do here without going active.''

"You got a solid fix?''

"Yeah. For the moment.''

"We could try a rescue now," said Hamstein.

"I don't think we should unless we get the call from him. We don't know enough. He hasn't asked for us.''

"Yeah," she said. "I suppose not." She pushed forward on the yoke and the ship began a slow descent. She turned it so that they were spiraling down, over New Washington.

She thought it would be good to be ready for Stone when he called for help. If he called.

"I don't like this," said Wilcox.

"But there is nothing else we can do," said Hamstein. "Not at the moment."

As the black-clad police closed in on him, Stone knew that the game was up. He grinned at them, searched for one who seemed to be the leader, and then repeated, "I'm Colonel Wallace Stone with the advance team from Earth."

"You are under arrest," said one of the men. "You will come with us."

"Certainly."

Stone was led away, surrounded by several of the police officers. Over his shoulder he saw that the men and women of the residence hall were beginning to filter back into the building, no longer interested in the events outside. Police stood near the doors watching as they did.

As they reached one of the hover cars, Stone said, "I would like an opportunity to call Colonel White, the leader of our landing team, and let him know what has happened."

"We'll take care of that at our headquarters," said one of the men.

"He's not that far from here."

"Routine procedure demands that we take you to our headquarters first," said the police officer.

But they didn't go to the police headquarters, but turned and drove toward the center of the city. Although there wasn't a sign on it, Stone knew that he was being taken into the medical center. White-clad workers, doctors, nurses, technicians, and orderlies swarmed the ground floor, many of them with red crosses on their coveralls.

"What are we doing here?" asked Stone.

"Routine. We want to make sure that you are healthy and that you weren't injured earlier."

"I'm fine," said Stone. "No injuries."

"A matter of routine."

They walked into the building, which was brightly lit. Every surface was white, clean, and antiseptic. A nurse hurried forward and asked, "Is this an emergency?"

"No. We'd just like a routine examination of this man. He might have been injured."

"Of course. Come with me."

Stone followed the nurse, dressed in a white coverall with a small red cross above the breast pocket. The nurse opened a door and gestured Stone inside. Stone sat in the chair and scanned the room quickly. There was only one exit and he knew that the police were watching it, probably half a dozen of them sitting just outside waiting for him to make a break.

The doctor entered and asked, "What seems to be the trouble here?"

"Nothing. Police brought me in."

"Ah." The doctor exited and two large orderlies entered followed by another doctor.

"We're going to give you a shot to calm you," announced the doctor.

Stone stood up and said, "I don't want any medication until I've had a chance to talk with my superior. I'm not authorized to accept medical treatment."

"This is only a mild sedative. Take the edge off, relax you, and then we can talk."

"No," said Stone.

"I'm afraid that you have no choice here. You will take the sedative now, or I will have you strapped to a table."

"I have my rights," said Stone, knowing that the bluff was weak.

The two orderlies separated, moving toward Stone from opposite sides of the room. The tactic was designed to confuse the victim, causing him to swing his head from one side to the other, watching the advancing men. But Stone knew the way to stop it. He faced the biggest of the men and kicked at the knee. He heard the bone break and saw bright red blood stain the front of the coverall.

As the man collapsed, Stone whirled to confront the

second orderly. The man launched himself toward Stone, his arms out, trying to snag Stone in a bear hug. Stone ducked under the arms, popped up behind the man, and whirled, punching him in the kidney. The man staggered forward, a hand out. He caught himself against the wall and turned toward Stone. His face was pasty white, surprised by the sudden violence of Stone's attack. He moaned low in his throat.

Stone waited, balanced on the balls of his feet, leaning forward slightly, watching the orderly. He'd forgotten about the doctor, not seeing her as a threat to him. She was small. A professional, who'd brought in two large men to subdue him if necessary. That had been Stone's mistake. He'd underestimated the situation.

The needle slid into his shoulder with a slight burning. He whirled, but it was too late. The needle broke, but the damage had been done. He took a step toward her as she jumped back, but the room began to swirl, the colors running together like a watercolor left in the rain. The lights brightened, the colors changing to white and then fading to black.

He reached out as if to grab her neck, but never made it. He fell forward and heard a voice, overly loud, say, "That'll keep him quiet until we're finished." That was the last thing he remembered.

CHAPTER

10

White, now in the company of Sister Susan, watched quietly as more children sang and danced for them. He saw the activities in front of him, but they didn't register on his brain. Instead he was thinking about what Titus had said before he had left. And he was thinking about Stone and what trouble he had gotten into. Although White didn't know Stone's exact job because of security, he knew that it had nothing to do with anthropology. He suspected it had to do with military intelligence.

Any problems generated by Stone would be solved, not by him but by the staff on the fleet. All he had to do was communicate the problem to the fleet and let them open the diplomatic channels. Of course, he couldn't initiate the dialogue until he received word from Stone.

Sister Susan sat next to him and made sure that his glass was never more than half empty. Someone was always there to add a little wine or liquor or water. While White watched the dancing children, Susan waved a hand and a man in green slipped closer, added some wine, and then disappeared quietly.

White picked up the glass, sipped the wine, and nodded his approval. He set the glass down and glanced at some of his staff. One man's head hung down, his chin on his chest, as if he had fallen asleep. No one seemed concerned that he had gone to sleep. The locals weren't insulted by it.

Pointing to the man, White leaned near Sister Susan and said, "We've had a very long day."

"We're nearly finished here," said Sister Susan, "and then you can return to your rooms for some rest."

"Good. We've another big day scheduled for tomorrow."

"Of course."

White noticed that another of his people had fallen asleep. She had laid her head on the table, cradling it in her arms. And next to her, another man was fighting a losing battle with his fatigue.

"This is odd," said White. He was going to wake all of them, but his body was leaden, almost too heavy for him to move. He wondered if there wasn't something in the atmosphere that made him think his body was too heavy. From the initial briefings, he knew that the gravity was just slightly higher than Earth normal but that shouldn't cause them any trouble.

He reached over and picked up the wineglass, taking a sip of it. He then leaned toward Sister Susan to tell her he was going to waken the others. He jerked once, realizing that he'd fallen asleep. He grinned at her and then she faded from sight and he was sound asleep.

As soon as the last of the guests had fallen asleep, Sister Susan stood up. The children stopped in mid-song and left the hall immediately without instruction. Adults, dressed in white, with small red crosses above their pockets, entered. Nurses gave each of the sleeping people a shot on the shoulder and then stretchers were unfolded. The sleeping people were loaded onto them quickly.

"Medicenter first," said Sister Susan, "and then return each of them to his or her room."

She left the hall, walking out into the cool night. She looked up into the sky, at the band of bright stars high overhead, and grinned. "Thought you'd put one over on us," she said to the invisible ships lost somewhere above her. "Looks like the trick is on you."

"Sister, we're ready now," said a white-clad woman.

"Then, sister, by all means proceed."

"Will you be coming along?"

At first she was going to say no but then changed her mind. "Yes, I'll come along."

They loaded the unconscious people into hover cars and drove them to the medicenter. Each was taken in and then down into the lower level. Each had a separate room where he or she was stretched out, an arm exposed. A doctor gave each person another shot and when it had taken effect, electrodes were attached to the head before being plugged into a small electronic unit hidden behind the bed.

Sister Susan moved among the various rooms watching as the operation progressed. She watched as the educational units were wheeled in, cables were attached to the electronic units, and the tapes began to roll. She watched as a psychologist monitored the progress of each of the tapes, and monitored the input for each of the "patients."

One of the doctors pulled her aside and said, "The influence over these people is going to be weak, at best. We'd need nearly a month of carefully controlled feed before we could expect anything like a ninety percent effective rate."

"Doctor," said Sister Susan, "all we hope to gain is an understanding by these outsiders of our system. Anything else is going to be pure luck. We don't want them inclined to look beyond the surface and this indoctrination will be sufficient to reach that goal."

"Won't they be suspicious after this?" he asked.

"No. Each will think that he or she had too much of a good time and passed out. All will be too embarrassed by it to mention it to anyone. If they ever discuss it among themselves, it will be long after they have left us in peace."

The doctor returned to his work. A moment later Brother Titus arrived and asked, "How did it go?"

"No problem. They just fell asleep one by one. Colonel White was going to wake a few of them, but was unable. They'll be back in their rooms before daybreak."

"Good."

"And you?"

"We have the spy now. He's been sedated and we'll begin the full course with him. He'll tell us everything we need to know in the next couple of days."

"Why don't they leave us alone?" asked Sister Susan. "That's all we want."

"They believe that they are helping us. How can we possibly be happy because our philosophies are not the same as theirs? Therefore, all they can do is try to help us see the light."

She shook her head slowly. "How deluded they are. You would think, intellectually, they would realize that ours is the better system. We don't have any of the problems they have been trying to solve for the last ten thousand years. Our society is peaceful."

Brother Titus waved a hand as if wiping the slate clean. He asked, "Are you able to take charge here?"

"Certainly. I got them down here, didn't I. I'll be able to get them back."

"Then I'll leave you," he said. "I've some other things I need to check on."

"Peace go with you, brother."

"Thank you, sister."

She watched as Titus hurried back to the escalator that would take him up to the ground floor. When he was out of sight, she turned and walked toward the closest of the doors. She pushed it open and leaned her head inside.

The patient was sitting up, eyes fully open but unseeing. Wires led from electrodes on the forehead, temples, right cheek, and back of the neck to the small machine sitting on a cart, hidden at the head of the bed. One technician was sitting in front of it, manipulating the dials. Another was watching the heart rate and respiration of the patient while a third just stared into the vacant eyes.

"It's progressing nicely. They use a similar technique for education," said one of the technicians. "There's almost no resistance to our programming. Makes our job that much easier."

"Good. Keep me informed of the progress."

"Surely, sister."

Sister Susan walked to the end of the hall and sat down to wait. It would only be an hour or so before each of the patients was finished and they would take them back to the hotel. Tomorrow would be interesting.

"I've lost him," said Wilcox. "Signal is completely gone now."

"You get a fix on his last position?"

"Yeah, for what good it'll do us."

"Oh-oh," said Hamstein. "We've got another problem coming up."

"What?" Wilcox leaned to the right and tried to see the instruments in front of Hamstein.

"We've got company. Two . . . no, three ships coming at us. Straight at us."

"What are you going to do?"

"I'm going to get the hell out of here right now. Rocky's on his own for the moment." She twisted around, flipped off one switch and activated another. She pushed a red cover out of the way and warned, "Prepare for immediate burn."

"We're breaking orbit."

''Hell, we're heading for the fleet,'' said Hamstein. ''Straight for the fleet.''

Wilcox activated the rearward-looking radar and saw three blips no more than fifty thousand feet behind them. Glancing at the infrared, they glowed brighter than the system's sun, meaning they were coming fast, engines still hot from the exhaust gases pushing them.

''Got them identified on screen,'' said Wilcox. ''Are we going to engage?''

''No. We're getting the hell out of here, as per our orders. We are not authorized to engage these people.''

''They're coming fast.''

''I hope you're strapped in tight. Here we go.''

She hit the button and the engines suddenly roared to life. Wilcox was slammed back into his seat, feeling as if an elephant had just rolled over his head to sit on his chest. His eyesight faded until it looked as if he were staring down a narrow tunnel with a dim light at the end. He could hear things around him but wasn't able to identify the sounds. For the moment he was confused.

The pressure let up suddenly and they jerked to the right and the pressure was back, heavier. He tried to see the instruments but they were nothing more than points of light glowing in the distance, the numbers on them blurred and unreadable. He couldn't tell what they said or if they were in trouble.

The nose seemed to drop and then pop up. The weight increased and then vanished. Wilcox reached out, as if to grab something to hold him in his seat.

''They're coming after us,'' said Hamstein. ''I think they want us to land.''

''We can't do that,'' said Wilcox, his voice sounding strange to him, as if he were talking at the bottom of a barrel.

''They're firing,'' said Hamstein. Her voice was now higher, filled with excitement.

Wilcox could see the screen giving him a rear view. The

enemy ships, he now thought of them as the enemy, were points of red racing right at them. He saw a single beam flash but it missed them.

"You see them?" asked Hamstein.

"Still coming up behind us."

"Sweep the area. Make sure that they don't have anyone else coming at us."

Wilcox touched one of the buttons and the radars began a 360-degree sweep. The only ships were the three chasing them. Nothing in front, to the sides, above or below them.

"Looks like it's only those three."

"Good."

Hamstein said, "We've got them now, I think. They're falling to the rear."

"They're firing again."

"Shields will hold."

Wilcox began to relax slightly. He saw that the distance to the enemy had increased now. The enemy was having trouble staying close as Hamstein worked to climb out of the planet's atmosphere. But then, as he watched, it looked as if the ships were beginning to break up. Lights sparkled around the front of the ship.

"Missiles," said Wilcox suddenly. "They've fired missiles at us."

"Okay," said Hamstein. Now she sounded calm. "Take the controls and hold us on this course. Don't do anything fancy now."

"Got it."

Hamstein spun her chair and glanced down at the missile warning display. A half-dozen small lights were heading straight for her on a corkscrewing course. She touched the keyboard of the targeting computer and then hit the fire button. For a moment nothing happened and then a single beam flared, reaching out to the closest of the missiles. It touched the nose, slipped away, and then came back. An instant later the missile detonated, disappearing in a bright flash of light. Now there were only five left on the display.

"That's one."

"Closing on us," said Wilcox.

"I see them."

Hamstein pressed her forehead against the upper ridge of the shield on the screen. She held the joystick in her right hand, feeling as if she were back in the simulator playing one of the many games designed to keep her sharp.

A second missile was hit and vanished. The computer launched one of its own antimissile missiles. The flight path, a bright streak on the screen, made no sense. It turned and jinked right and left as it tried to intercept another of the enemy missiles. It collided with it and the missile spun off into space finally detonating into a brilliant but tiny burst of light.

"Another salvo," said Wilcox.

"Can we outrun them?"

Wilcox used his computer and said, "Depends on the fuel consumption of them. Probably. Maybe."

"That's not what I want to hear."

"I've got a fourth ship," said Wilcox. "Just appeared. Seventy-five thousand feet below us, but coming up at mock nine. He's moving."

"Shit," she said. She didn't look at any of the other screens. She was watching the missiles. Another vanished as the computer hit it, destroying its fellow in the explosion. The last from the first salvo sputtered out and began a long, gentle arc as it fell back toward the planet's surface.

"Status of those other missiles?"

"Still closing but not rapidly."

The ship rocked then, first right and then left. "What in the hell was that?"

"Beam from the planet's surface," said Wilcox. "Got the ion trail spotted."

"We can't take much more of this."

"We could put a missile into that ground station," said Wilcox.

"No," said Hamstein. "Orders were quite clear."

One of the enemy missiles penetrated the outer computer defenses and detonated no more than a thousand meters from the ship. The bright flash overwhelmed the screens, blanking them for the moment.

When they cleared, Wilcox was horrified. "There are another three ships up here, coming at us. They've got an angle on us. We're in it deep."

Hamstein turned and grabbed the controls. "I've got it. Hang on."

She pushed the stick forward and added power. They began a rapid dive, toward the missiles that had been racing at them. That broke the first of the radar and infrared locks. She turned to the right and then pulled up suddenly, climbing again, but now with more speed than before. Ten seconds later she entered another dive, trying to confuse the enemy fighters that now seemed to fill the sky.

"Where in the hell did they all come from?"

The beam from the ground raked them again, buffeting the craft. Wilcox shouted, "Screens collapsing. We're beginning to lose it."

"Shit," said Hamstein. She pulled back again and began a shallow climb. She rolled right and then left, jerking the controls to throw off the locks of the enemy missiles and to defeat the beam weapons on the planet's surface.

"Should we alert the fleet," said Wilcox.

"Wait one," said Hamstein. "I'm not done yet. Not by a long shot."

"They're hostile," said Wilcox. "Let's treat them that way now."

"Wait one," she snapped again.

Now they were in a rapid climb with the engines at full power. She was trying to get above the service ceilings of the various planes and ships coming at them. She watched as the fuel in her tanks drained away, looking as if they had opened a hole in them.

She saw that they were pulling away from all the enemy craft and backed off the throttle, trying to conserve some of the fuel now. She saw two of the missiles detonate as they ran out of fuel and energy and exploded. They were too far away to cause any trouble for Hamstein.

"I think we've about got it made," she said.

"I don't know," said Wilcox.

The ground-based beam fired again, but the power seemed to have doubled. It raked the ship, destroying the remaining screens. The rear of the ship, near the engine baffles, began to superheat.

"We're going to lose it," said Hamstein as she watched the temperature gauge climb.

But the beam faded and disappeared. The rear of the ship began to cool, the temperature dropping away from the danger zone. The enemy ships were still falling back and the last of the missiles had exploded harmlessly far below them.

"Okay," said Hamstein. "I think we're clear."

But then the beam caught them again and with the shields melted away, the rear of the ship superheated. The metal collapsed and flowed like water down the side of a pitcher. The main engines failed and Hamstein knew that there was now nothing she could do.

"We're going down," she said. "Make the Mayday call."

Wilcox sat still for a moment and then hit the button that activated the recorded emergency message. Glancing at Hamstein, he said, "Mayday call activated."

"Good. Now hang on."

CHAPTER

11

Price was alerted by a quiet buzzing at the hatch. He rolled onto his back, lifted his hand so that he could look at his watch, and wondered why it was always necessary to wake him in the middle of the night. Why couldn't things go wrong in the early afternoon.

He touched a button and said, "Yes?"

"Captain Price? Colonel wants to see you in the conference room at your convenience."

"I assume," said Price, "that my convenience is now and not in the morning."

"Yes, sir. Sorry, sir."

Price rolled over, closed his eyes as if he were going back to sleep, and then levered himself up. He sat on the side of the cot, his feet on the deck, and took a deep breath. He tried not to think about the fact it was almost three and that there was little chance that he'd be able to get back to bed. He tried not to think about how he'd been up until midnight, thinking that he'd have the chance to sleep in. Instead, he pushed himself up and padded to the small sink and let the water trinkle into it so that he could splash it on his face. He could feel the beginning of the dull ache behind his eyes that meant he'd be in trouble by six. Lack of sleep did that to him.

He straightened up, wiped his face, and then put on his uniform. He walked to the hatch, stepped through, and then hurried toward the conference room.

As he reached the conference room, he saw Coollege. "Morning, Jackknife," he said. "Got you too."

"Yeah. You have any idea what this is about?"

"Only that it's going to be bad news. Either Rocky got himself into some kind of trouble or Hamstein did."

"You know that for a fact?"

"Nope. I'm just guessing, but that's the way things go around here. Besides, what else could it be." He moved toward the hatch, let it iris open, and then bowed slightly, letting Coollege enter in front of him.

The Colonel was sitting at the head of the table, his eyes closed as if resting. He opened them as Price and Coollege entered. "Have a seat. We've got trouble."

Price shot a glance at Coollege as he sat down. "What's going on?"

"We've lost contact with Sergeant Stone," said the Colonel. "Hamstein was attacked and knocked down and our landing team missed their last check-in."

Price fought down the urge to laugh. It was worse than he thought. Everything possible had gone wrong. He rubbed a hand over his chin and realized that he needed to shave.

"Reports are in front of you," said the Colonel. "Take a look at it and tell me what you think."

Price took a look at the computer printouts. He flipped the page and read the last of it. He sat back, waited for Coollege, and then said, "Looks like Rocky slipped up."

"Probably, but then, that's not the biggest problem," said the Colonel.

"No. Rocky should be able to work his way out of it. I can't believe that he'd get himself caught that quickly.

There really isn't anything here to suggest that the landing team is in trouble. Just a single missed check-in. That'll probably change in the morning.''

Price stopped talking. Both those ideas were minor. But then there was the attack on Hamstein, there was no way to rationalize it away.

"What about the attack on Hamstein?'' asked Coollege.

"Protests have been lodged through the diplomatic channels, but it is late at night. Besides, I know what the answer will be. They'll stonewall at first and then say that Hamstein was in violation of their sovereignty. It will be our fault that Hamstein was attacked. Or rather her fault.''

"She and Wilcox are down?''

The Colonel took a deep breath. "We have had no reports from them since we received their Mayday call. They must be down somewhere on the planet's surface. We don't know if they survived the crash.''

Price leaned forward and propped his head in his hands. He massaged his temples, trying to think, but could only concentrate on the dull throbbing caused by a lack of sleep. He was at a loss to make any kind of intelligent suggestion.

Coollege on the other hand was sharp. "What we have right now is Rocky in custody, Hamstein and Wilcox down, probably for violating their airspace, and a failure by the landing team to report. Nothing that suggests a hostile intent on their part. All can be explained as a response to our actions.''

"At the moment,'' agreed the Colonel.

Price stared at the top of the table and said, "We need to get down there ourselves and see what's going on. We . . .'' Suddenly he fell silent, his training finally taking over. Never give anyone a hint of the plans because you never really knew who would pass on the information. It could be as innocent as someone speaking out of turn or as deadly as a mole in the organization. He didn't know when the room had last been swept for listening devices.

Covering, Price said, "Maybe have Lieutenant Coollege drop down tomorrow to check on things."

"You mean contact the landing team?" asked the Colonel.

"No, sir. Slip down and just listen to what is happening. We shouldn't make contact with anyone on the surface right now."

The Colonel closed his leather-bound folder. "I'll authorize anything you feel necessary. Coordinate with my assistant in the morning."

"Yes, sir."

The Colonel stood and walked from the conference room. When he was gone, Coollege said, "You're really going to send me down there alone?"

"Of course," said Price. He almost added that he would be following in a matter of minutes, but decided not to say anything. Suddenly he was paranoid as hell, fearing that the conference room might be bugged. Too many odd things had happened too fast.

Hamstein had pulled Wilcox from the wreckage of their ship just as the flames had spread from under the nose to engulf the cockpit area. Heavy black smoke marked the crash site like a beacon.

She had fought to get them down in one piece, working the controls, throttles, and engines as they had first plummeted through the atmosphere and finally begun to glide. She hadn't cared about the crash site, only that she slow the rate of descent because they were dropping too fast. When she shallowed that out, she was able to glance at the terrain avoidance radar and the computer-generated display of the surface. There were a dozen long, level fields for her to aim at. She found one and began the approach.

Wilcox had sat next to her quietly, hanging on to his seat, his knuckles as white as his face. He was frightened, but didn't say a word, having confidence in Hamstein. She would get them down safely, if it was at all possible.

The enemy ships had given chase, following her through the cloud cover, but none of them swooped in for the kill. They monitored the progress of the ship as it fell as if to make sure it wasn't a trick. When it was apparent that Hamstein was going to crash, that she wasn't going to suddenly pull up in a climb, they peeled away.

They had touched down at the far end of the plain, skidded across it, bouncing high a couple of times and then crashing back. Bits of the ship broke off leaving a trail of debris in a gouge almost a mile long. When they finally came to rest, Hamstein popped the emergency hatch that blew out the door, scrambled to it, and then pulled Wilcox free. Fire had erupted but it hadn't spread too far. As soon as she got Wilcox to safety, she turned, but the flames had finally engulfed most of the ship. She wouldn't be returning to grab the survival gear or radio.

Watching the ship burn, she said, almost to herself, "I guess we're on our own now."

"Fleet knows we're down," said Wilcox weakly. "They'll be out to rescue us."

Hamstein looked up into the brightening of the sky, searching for either rescue craft or enemy fighters. She saw neither.

"We're on our own for the moment," she repeated. "Fleet couldn't have anyone here for an hour or so."

Wilcox laid back, looking up into the sky. "We just have to sit tight."

Hamstein nodded but thought of all the training she'd had over the last few years. When down in hostile territory, the first thing to be done was to get away from the crash. Move as far and as fast as possible because the enemy would use it as the focus for the search. Of course, there wasn't a real enemy yet. The locals might have shot them out of the sky, but that could be for violating their airspace. No state of war existed, nor one was likely to exist in the immediate future. She didn't have to worry about becoming a POW.

Still, Hamstein liked the general philosophy of getting the

hell away from the burning wreck. "You feel up to moving around a little bit?" she asked.

Wilcox, now with an arm over his eyes to shade them, said, "Can't we rest for a few minutes?"

Hamstein nodded and sat down beside him. She studied the ground under her, poking at it with a small twig. In the distance she heard the sound of an aircraft and looked up to see a helicopter racing toward the plume of smoke. It was suddenly too late to attempt an escape.

"Hang on," she said. "We've got someone coming."

"Why don't you get out?" said Wilcox. "They'll find me and you'll have a chance to escape."

Hamstein thought about it. Wilcox wasn't hurt that badly and there would be someone around to help him when the chopper arrived. If she managed to escape, she might be able to provide information for others who might be required to follow. She would become an important intelligence asset.

"Okay," she said reluctantly. "If you're sure you'll be fine."

"Go," said Wilcox.

Hamstein stood up and cupped a hand over her eyes to shield them. The enemy helicopter was still a long way off. If they had any kind of sophisticated sensing equipment, they'd find her in a minute, if they looked. But she still had to try to escape.

She ran across the open ground, bending low. She found a shallow ditch and dropped into it, crawling along the bottom to stay out of sight. In the tall grass, she was shielded from the helicopter. If she stretched out on the damp bottom, motionless, they might not see her and leave her behind if they made a quick survey.

The sound of the chopper filled the morning. The rotor blades popped as they slowed and came to hover, over Wilcox, she hoped. She wanted to turn to watch but knew the slightest movement in the grass could give her away.

She wouldn't move until she was sure that the helicopter was gone.

She lay facedown, breathing slowly, the odor of the wet dirt filling her nostrils. The sound of the helicopter changed as it settled to the ground. She heard voices and heard Wilcox trying to convince them that he had been all alone in the ship. The people from the chopper spread out in a quick search, but gave up after only a couple of minutes. Wilcox shouted something but she couldn't understand the words. The sound of the chopper's engine changed then and a moment later it lifted off again. It seemed to hang in the air, as if making one last survey of the crash site, and then began to fly back to the city. The sound receded slowly until it was little more than an insectile buzz that finally faded away. It was quiet then. Extraordinarily quiet.

Hamstein pushed herself to her knees and then stood up. There was no one around her. There was nothing to see overhead. The plume of black smoke from the burning ship had thinned, but still marked the spot.

Hamstein climbed out of the ditch and walked back to where she had left Wilcox. The grass had been flattened by the chopper. She could see marks on the ground where it had set down. Wilcox was gone as she had known he would be. They had taken him with them. He must have convinced them that he was alone because no one searched for her very long.

She sat down again and looked at the ground between her feet. "Now what do I do?" she asked out loud.

There was no answer.

CHAPTER 12

Stone felt like he was about to wake up. He knew that he was asleep and that he'd had a number of bad dreams, but now he was becoming aware of the situation around him, outside of the dreams. Sleep faded and he opened his eyes to see the antiseptic brightness of a modern hospital. He remembered that he had been sick, or thought that he had been sick, but couldn't remember the symptoms of the disease.

"How are we feeling?" asked a nurse who was standing over him, holding his wrist as if to take his pulse. She was staring down, into his eyes.

"Better." The word seemed to stick in his throat. He wanted something to drink to wash the muck from his tongue.

The nurse released his wrist and picked up a cup with a bent straw in it. She held it out for him and said, "Want something to drink?"

Stone wondered if she had read his mind as he sucked down the water. Finished, he laid back, against the pillows,

and took a deep breath. He tried to remember what he had
been doing the night before. He tried to remember what he
had been doing for the last week. The memories were
shrouded in fog. All he knew was that he had been sick,
acting as an individual, and working against the people of
Bolton's Planet. He was suddenly overwhelmed by a feeling
of remorse. He'd acted badly and yet they were doing
everything they could to help him.

"I'm so sorry," he croaked.

The nurse patted his hand. "You've been sick, but you're
better now. Relax. Forget everything that happened before.
It no longer matters."

"I tried to . . ." He knew that he had tried something
bad the night before, but the act was lost in the fog. It was
wrong, but he couldn't remember why.

"I'll get the doctor and he'll be able to help you," said
the nurse.

"Thank you." A feeling of gratitude swelled through
him and he knew he would never be able to repay the
kindness shown him.

The nurse left and Stone tried to sort through his
memories. Last night was gone. He knew that he worked
with a fleet in space, and that he had been on some kind of
assignment. But that was all he remembered. He didn't
understand the society of Bolton's Planet or how it was all
interrelated and interconnected. He knew it was a peaceful
society without crime, disease, hunger, or want. Everyone
was happy in the society. No one was ignored or abused. It
was a good place to live.

The doctor tapped on the door and asked, "You mind if
I come in?"

"No, Doctor. Please."

The doctor looked at the computer screen set on a small
table near Stone and read the information stored on it. He
nodded once and asked, "How are you feeling?"

"Confused," said Stone.

"To be expected. You took quite a jolt on the head last

night when you fell on the escalator. Fought with the nurses and technicians when they brought you in here.''

''Oh,'' said Stone, again awash in remorse. ''I hope that no one was injured.''

''No. Everyone is fine. In fact, everyone has been asking about you. Gave us all quite a fright.''

''I'm sorry.''

''There is nothing to be sorry about,'' said the doctor. ''Your job now is to get well so that you can return to your friends on the fleet.''

''What if I want to stay here?'' asked Stone.

''Well, I'm sure that we could work something out if that was what you really wanted. But I think that is something you should think about later. Right now I just want you to relax and take it easy.''

''Of course,'' said Stone.

''The nurse will be along later with some medication for you. Please take it all as it is prescribed. If you suddenly feel better and think you don't need something, you could, in the long run, hinder your recovery.''

''Yes, Doctor. Thank you.''

''Thank our leaders for their generosity.''

When the doctor left, Stone rolled to his side and looked down at the cold tile of the floor. He tried to remember what he had been doing the night before but couldn't. Even with the hints given to him by the doctor, the night was a blank. He'd been engaged in activity that was wrong, but he just couldn't remember what it was. Maybe, as he got better, he would be able to remember more of the night.

Before he had a chance to worry about it, his eyes grew heavy and he knew that he was about to go to sleep. He felt safe and calm, a feeling that he didn't remember having much in the past. He hoped that it would continue.

Coollege stood in the ready room just off the shuttle bay and looked at herself in the full-length mirror. She wore an off-white robe with green piping on it. Her hair had been dyed black and trimmed short. She wasn't sure that she recognized the woman who looked back at her.

Price entered, studied her, and said, "You should be able to pass."

"Hell, this will never work," she said. "I don't know half of what I need to."

"Your job is to observe. Walk around slowly, nod greetings, and you'll be fine."

She shook her head. "I'm not convinced that I understand what I'm doing."

"Gathering data, pure and simple. Nothing else. Just observe from an insider's position. With Stone's mission an obvious failure, we're going to see what we can learn from this. We need some additional data."

"Sure."

Price laughed. "I think the thing that we're all forgetting is that this is a friendly planet. I mean, they're not going to arrest you for spying and then shoot you out of hand. Tell them you were just interested in seeing how things worked on the inside. They might not appreciate the invasion of their privacy, but that's about all it is. It's certainly not a capital offense."

"Why don't I feel better about this?" asked Coollege.

"I don't know. Why don't you?"

"When are you coming down?" she asked, changing the subject then.

"Probably not for a couple of days. With everyone gone from the intel office, someone has to mind the store."

"Nice duty."

"Double duty," said Price. "I have to cover for everyone and everything. You know how the Colonel gets."

She turned away from the mirror and looked right at him. "Just what in the hell is going on?"

"I don't know. I thought the clues were on that cube we worked so hard to recover but that doesn't seem to be the case. No clues there. Just someone talking to the governmental leaders who probably shouldn't have had access to them, but that certainly doesn't mean anything."

Coollege took a deep breath and exhaled. "I suppose I'd better get going."

"Emma, be careful on this. We've already lost Rocky. I can't afford to lose you too."

"Your words make my heart hammer," she said.

"You know what I mean."

"That's the problem," she said. "I know exactly what you mean." Then she smiled. "I'll be in touch."

Price watched her exit the ready room. He didn't follow her, not wanting to provide anyone outside the intell office any additional information. He knew that her wearing the robe would alert anyone to her mission if they saw her. It was a strange game to be playing. Half security measures so that anyone watching would think that the mission was progressing according to some kind of a plan.

White awoke in his own bed in his own room in the guest quarters of the city. He remembered nothing of getting there. He could remember the reception the night before with dancing and singing children, dozens of kinds of food, and lots of alcoholic beverages. He remembered seeing some of his people asleep at their tables and he remembered thinking that he should awaken them, but that was all he remembered. And those memories weren't too clear, shrouded in a haze that was difficult for him to penetrate.

He swung his legs out of bed and then heard a sound in the bathroom off to the right. He froze, wondering who would be in there at that time of the morning. Then he stood, wanting to confront the intruder, but his head began to swim, the room began to swirl, and he was afraid that he was going to fall down. He sat heavily, with a grunt.

"Are you awake?" called a feminine voice from inside the bathroom.

White didn't respond. He gripped the sheets hoping that

he wouldn't be suddenly sick. He closed his eyes, which helped for the moment, but when he heard movement close, he opened them.

"Are you feeling ill?" Sister Susan stood in front of him, nude. Her hair had been loosened and hung to her shoulders. She held a towel in one hand but made no move to cover herself with it.

"What happened?" asked White.

"I believe you consumed a little more wine than you should have. I brought you here to recover."

"You're . . ."

Sister Susan smiled broadly and said, "You seem to have become very affectionate. I've never seen so many hands on one person."

"Oh, my God," said White.

"Please don't concern yourself. I must admit that I didn't find the idea repugnant myself. I helped you remove my robe. I was a willing participant."

White groaned and cradled his head in his hands. He knew that he had compromised himself. Any negotiations that were to be conducted would now have this taint on them. He was useless to the fleet. As soon as he could, he should report to the fleet and have them dispatch another diplomat.

"No one has to know," said Sister Susan. "It was something that we shared privately."

"Part of the welcome to your world?" asked White weakly.

"If you want to reduce it to that," she said, "then, yes, part of the welcome. I believe it had a little more emotion involved." She slipped around and sat beside him, an arm on his shoulder.

White stood up suddenly, felt the room tilt and saw it fade, but he stood still waiting for his head to clear. He finally took a step toward the balcony where he could look out, into the city that was beginning to stir.

"I could go if I make you too uncomfortable," said Sister Susan.

Without looking back at her, White said, "Maybe it would be better if you did."

"Of course. I'll see you for lunch then?"

"I'm not sure that would be a good idea," said White. "Not now." He hesitated and then added, "The lunch isn't a good idea right now."

"I meant that the schedule calls for a luncheon today. We'll all be there."

"Ah."

Sister Susan stood up and walked toward him. She leaned against him, pressing herself forward. "There really is nothing to worry about."

"Please," said White.

She released him and retreated across the room. White turned and said, "You have to understand. We are supposed to remain . . . we are not supposed to fraternize with our hosts. It's just not the proper form."

"Our ways are different," said Sister Susan. "If we can give pleasure to one another, then we do so. There is no guilt to be attached and it should not interfere with your mission here on our planet."

"I'm only suggesting that it might become a problem. I hope that you understand."

Sister Susan scooped her robe from the floor where it had landed the night before and slipped it over her head. She smoothed it over her hips, adjusting it slightly. She slipped her feet into her sandals and then smiled broadly.

"If you would like to get together again, privately, I would enjoy it. No strings attached. No favors asked. No one the wiser if we please each other. I just enjoy your company," she said. She reached out and touched his chin, looking deeply into his eyes.

White took a step back and said, "Thank you." He didn't know what else to say and had learned long ago that the only mistake to be made in that situation was to try to think of something witty. The best thing he could do was say nothing.

Sister Susan walked to the door, opened it, turned and waved, and then slipped into the hall. White breathed a sigh of relief, figuring that he would now do everything in his power to avoid being alone with her again. He'd already made too many mistakes.

He walked out on the balcony to look down into the city. The people were already up and moving, dressed in robes and coveralls, each walking at the same pace as all the others, smiling obediently, nodding to each other, and waving to friends. A very peaceful, gentle society that posed no threat to him or anyone else in the galaxy.

As he sat down on the plastic chair he realized for the first time that he was nude. He had carried on a conversation with a woman, sent her from his bed and room, and had not realized that he was standing there as bare as she. He laughed out loud at the irony of the situation and then hurried back into his room.

The day promised to be a long one. Especially with what had happened during the night. He hoped that she would be discreet about the events of the past but somehow felt that it had all been part of the grand design. The enemy, if these people were the enemy, were working very hard to compromise him and his staff.

White picked up his clothes and folded them, putting them on the foot of the bed. He stretched, his back popping as he did. Suddenly he realized that he felt very good. He felt . . . he was . . . elated with the situation.

These people were not the enemy. They were friends. They were helpful, courteous, and friendly. There was nothing for him to worry about. His mission would continue and he would return to the fleet, reporting that there was nothing happening on the planet that deserved their attention.

He walked into the bathroom, turned on the shower, and

then adjusted the spray so that it was needle-sharp and ice-cold. He'd start off the day with a cold shower, and he would then be ready to face anything they threw at him. The day would be perfect. It had already started out that way.

CHAPTER

13

Coollege, concealed in a large crate wheeled into a storage area, listened until she was sure that there were no workers around. Then, carefully, she peeled open the crate from the inside and slipped out, sealing it again quickly. There was no evidence that anyone had been hiding inside.

She worked her way among the crates, following the yellow lines painted on the floor until she spotted a door. She walked to it, put an ear against it, and finally just opened it. She stepped out, onto a ramp that would lead her into the spaceport proper. If she could get beyond the barriers there, she would have landed on the planet illegally and there would be no record of her arrival. She could roam around without the authorities knowing that she was there.

When that area was clear, she slipped out, walked rapidly up the ramp, and opened another door. As she crossed a room, someone shouted at her. "Hey, sister, you're not supposed to be in here."

Coollege stopped and turned, smiling. "I'm sorry, brother, but I seem to have gotten lost."

"Let me help you." The man in red coveralls hurried forward, took her arm, and led her to the closest door. "Through here and then turn right. You'll find yourself right back in the terminal."

"Thank you, brother."

Coollege entered into the spaceport proper and fell in with the crowd as they moved toward the main terminal exit. They walked past a number of black-clad police officers who paid no attention to anyone. Coollege glanced at them with idle curiosity and then looked away, focusing her attention on the large windows at the front of the terminal. They marked her destination.

She reached the entrance and walked out into the sunshine. She wanted to look behind her, to see if the police were following, but her training told her that was the quickest way to give her away. She was an innocent woman, entering New Washington, who had business in the downtown complexes. She didn't have any reason to suspect the police would be interested in her.

A hover car pulled up, settled to the ground, and the driver exited to help his passengers unload their lugguage as they entered the terminal. When the cab was empty, the driver asked her, "Do you want a ride into town?"

"Yes, brother. Thank you."

She climbed in, sat by the window, and then looked out, at the terminal building. There were more police standing around it, almost ringing it, but they seemed to have no interest in any of the arriving passengers. They were interested in the security of the structure and that was it.

When the hover car was filled, the driver climbed in, started it up, and drove toward the capital. There was no hurry, no crowd or traffic, no crush of individual cars. Another hover car tried to enter the traffic way and the driver slowed, waving at his opposite number. No one tried to beat the other to the ramp.

They entered the downtown and the driver pulled to the curb. "Here we are," he announced, turning to smile at her.

Coollege climbed down and joined the people as they walked among the buildings. Unlike them, she had no destination. She was there to observe and see what she could learn. No one paid any attention to her. They nodded to her and called her sister, but that was the extent of their interest.

She walked into a building and watched the people there. She sat down and waited. She wasn't sure what she was looking for, but was feeling good. She'd gotten into the city without anyone suspecting her.

"Good morning, sister," said a man. "Is there some way that I might be of assistance?"

Coollege shook her head and said, "No, brother. I am waiting for a friend."

"Does he live here?"

"Yes." As soon as she said it, she knew that it was wrong. That was something that could be checked easily. Never, but never do anything or say anything that could be easily checked. It was the quickest way to be discovered.

"His name?"

"He'll be along shortly. I'm just sitting here," said Coollege. "I'll be going in a few minutes."

"Please, sister, sit as long as you desire. Good day."

She watched him walk away and knew that she had better get out. But she also knew that if she moved too quickly, it would arouse more suspicion. It made an interesting problem for her.

"Sister," said another voice from behind her. "Could you come with me?"

She looked up at a man dressed in a yellow coverall. He was a stocky man with dark hair and perfect teeth.

"I'm waiting for a friend," she said.

"Of course, you are, but I'm afraid that I must insist. You can return quickly."

"My friend will be here any moment. I don't want to miss him."

"And he'll wait for you, I'm sure."

"All right, brother," she said, standing. "Where are we going?"

"Quick interview," said the man. He took her hand and led her from the building.

For an hour or so, Hamstein wasn't sure what to do. She had moved away from the wreckage of her ship and then had dropped to the ground to rest. With the survival radio gone, with the ship burned, and with Wilcox captured, she wasn't sure what she should do. Everything that she could think of was predicated on the idea that the fleet would know that she was down, that they knew where she was down, and that there was someplace for her to escape to. Not here. The enemy was everywhere.

Finally she climbed to her feet and began to walk, sticking close to the tree line, searching the sky overhead. She listened for the sound of a returning chopper. No one seemed to care that she was out there. No one seemed to know that she was out there.

She stopped after an hour and sat on a log. Her options were limited. And then she saw an obvious solution. Walk into New Washington and search for Colonel White and his landing team. They would be able to communicate with the fleet and get her a lift back up there.

She began to walk again, happy that she now had a destination. In the distance she heard voices and walked toward the sound. She came over a small hill and saw a wide, graveled roadway stretching off into the distance. People on bikes were riding on the edges and others were walking down the center. The pace was slow, leisurely. Hamstein stood watching for a moment, and then strolled down the hill and joined those heading toward New Washington.

"Morning, sister," said a man who approached from the opposite direction. "You're looking a little worn out. May I be of help?"

"I got lost. Separated from my group. But it's fine now. I've found the road."

The man held out a container. "I have some water if you'd like it."

"Yes, thank you," she said.

"There's a rest zone ahead. Maybe you should sit down there. Maybe call for some help."

"No," said Hamstein. "I just want to find my friends now. I'll be fine."

"Certainly, sister." The man took his container back and then dropped away, joining the group he had been with earlier.

Hamstein turned and saw them all staring at her. One of the men pointed. Hamstein sped up, trying to get away from that group.

She turned a corner and saw the rest area only fifty meters in front of her. A half-dozen police stood there surveying the people as they passed. It was obvious they were searching for someone special. Hamstein stopped suddenly and a woman walked into her.

"Sorry, sister."

Hamstein nodded her response. She took a step to the rear. One of the police saw her and said something to the others. They began to advance. Hamstein thought about running and realized that it would do no good. She had been seen, her clothes didn't match those of the others, and now the police knew she was there. In a minute there would be a chopper in the air approaching. There was no way she could avoid the helicopter. Rather than run, she stood there and waited for them to reach her.

"You'll have to come with us, sister," said one of the police officers.

"Only if you have something to eat."

"As soon as we reach the station you'll receive food and drink. That and medical attention if you need it."

Hamstein said, "That'll be fine. And you'll have to alert

my fleet that I crashed. They'll want to pick me up soon as they can.''

"Of course. Just as soon as we finish with our work." Hamstein relaxed. "Thank you."

White was surprised that three of his staff had not made the morning meeting. His head hurt and the lights seemed overly bright, but that was no excuse for them to fail in their duties. He sent for them and was told that they had not spent the night in their rooms. They had vanished.

"What in the hell is going on?" he demanded. But then he thought of Sister Susan and that she had spent the night with him. It was possible that his missing people had spent the night with locals in their rooms. Vanished might not be the right word. They were missing for the moment but would probably turn up in an hour or so.

"Any of them call or leave a message?" asked White.

"No, Colonel," said Hall.

"Do we know where any of them are?"

"No, Colonel. I have taken the liberty of having our hosts check with their people but that is taking a little time. Besides, this is not my duty," said Hall. "Your coordinator is among the currently missing."

White groaned quietly and tried to think his way through the problem though the throbbing in his head made it difficult to concentrate. He wasn't concerned, he decided, knowing that his people were safe somewhere in New Washington. He knew they hadn't been mugged, kidnapped, or murdered. Such things didn't happen on Bolton's Planet.

And then he wondered why he was so confident about that. He had nothing but good feelings for the society and the people in it, but he couldn't figure out why. He'd read all the propaganda before he had set foot on the planet, but he hadn't been convinced then. Every planet, every country, and every city that he had ever visited had tried to put the best face possible on their society. The briefings usually covered some of the seamier sides. But all those doubts were gone. He felt good about the society. He felt that nothing wrong could happen to any of his people.

"They can't have gotten too far, Colonel," said Hall.

"No. Not without transportation and leaving a clue."

"We'll know something in a few minutes I'm sure."

A woman in a blue coverall entered and announced, "We have been unable to locate your people, but we are continuing to search." She sat down in the closest chair and added, "We have spoken to everyone who was at the reception last night but I'm afraid that we learned nothing new."

"Thank you," said White. Turning to his staff, he asked, "Who is missing?"

"Colonel Stone. We haven't seen him since late yesterday afternoon. He was not at the reception last night."

"And?"

"Mr. Robert Reinert and Dr. Eileen Stouffer."

White sat quietly until the woman in the blue coverall stood up and left. Then, lowering his voice, he asked, "Is there anything special about those people?"

"No, Colonel. Normal members of a landing team into a nonthreatening environment. Experts in culture and in finance. I think you know that Colonel Stone was more than just a military expert."

White nodded but could see no pattern. Finance was of no importance on Bolton's Planet. Their economic system didn't allow for a finance manager. The cultural anthropologist might have seen something under the surface that others might not have recognized. The real worry was Stone who was there supposedly to access the military capability of the planet's military and police forces.

"I want nothing else done," said White, "until our missing people are located. I will not stand for the disappearance of our people with some flimsy excuse that they can't be found. Not in this society."

"Yes, sir."

White then rested his head on his arms and wished that he had remembered what happened when he drank. Each morning after, as he sat nursing his hangover, he promised himself that he would remember. But the next time he forgot, sucking down the alcohol as if there were no tomorrow. Maybe he should just abstain. That would solve the problem once and for all. The pounding in his head made it difficult to think.

There was something bothering him about the whole episode, but he couldn't put his finger on it. There was a question that he should ask or a demand he should make, but it was lost in the throbbing in the back of his head.

"I'll inform the fleet about the problem," said Hall.

He was going to suggest another course of action, but didn't know what it should be. Finally he said, "You do that. "Maybe they'll have an answer for us."

"Yes, sir."

CHAPTER

14

The news was bad and getting worse. Everyone who was being sent down to Bolton's Planet was disappearing. Those whose mission was covert and who might have gotten themselves into trouble were gone, as were a few members of the diplomatic group. Everyone on the planet seemed concerned, they claimed they were doing everything possible to find the missing people, but no progress was being made.

Price, sitting alone in the intell office, monitoring what he could from the planet, was not impressed with the efforts. To him, the protestations of the planetary officials rang hollow. Father Bob sounded as if he was offering the same kind of feeble excuses that the government offered their own people. The difference was, Price was a cynic, not believing anything anyone had to say without proof being offered. It was his impression that the planet's government including Father Bob didn't care how many people disappeared.

Using the ship's mainframe, he called up what information he could, but there had been nothing added to it since he and Coollege had reviewed it in depth the day before. All he knew was that there was a planet-wide government and a single society that was lacking in the characteristics that made people human.

Sitting there, looking at the screens, at the information scrolling across them, he realized the one thing that everyone had ignored. Those on the planet's surface seemed to have a pipeline into the fleet. He'd had the first inklings the night before, when the colonel was briefing them, but he hadn't understood all the implications. He'd written it off to the normal paranoia that was an occupational hazard of intelligence.

But now, he realized, Bolton's Planet had been ready for everything, responding to threats from the fleet before they appeared. They had even discovered Hamstein's ship that should have been invisible to planetary radars and sensors, if they didn't know something was there to find and they didn't know exactly where to look.

Price sat back in his chair, rubbed the sweat from his face, and understood the real problem for the first time. There was someone on the ship who was feeding information to the ground on a regular basis. A burst transmission with coded information might last most of a second and if no one was searching for it, no one would detect it. It could be disguised as any one of a number of normal radiations coming from any of the ships in the fleet.

Suddenly he felt his belly grow cold. He reached up, touched the controls, and tried to find Coollege. She would be on the surface, should have cleared the terminal, and would be in the city.

But the signal that should have been there was not. The signal to help trace her through the city was gone. It had been a risk to have her wired that way, but too many other strange things had happened. Price had wanted to be able to find her as quickly and as easily as possible. But the computers failed to locate her. She had suddenly fallen off the face of the planet.

Price didn't know how to react for the moment. He sat there, staring at the computer screen, trying to wish a response from it. He kept wondering if he had done something wrong, pushed the wrong button, coded the wrong word, but every time he checked, the same response appeared. The signal was gone. Coollege was gone.

It was possible that the battery had failed. Or the unit had failed. Or that there was some kind of interference between his receiver and her transmitter. There were a dozen such answers, but Price knew they were all wrong. The equipment hadn't failed and there was nothing between him and her that would eliminate the signal. Something had already gone wrong on the planet.

He stood up and walked around the console. He stood facing the bulkhead, staring at it as if the answers to his questions might be written on it. "Okay," he said. "The problem is that someone here is giving information to the enemy. Now I have to take action without telling a soul."

He didn't understand why he felt compelled to speak out loud. He fell silent and tried to think of the way to arrange it. He could always steal a ship and fly himself to Bolton's Planet. The theft might be reported and the spy, whoever it was, might figure it out. But the odds were that there would be no general discussion of a stolen ship, not until the thief was caught.

He looked at the empty office. Everyone who was normally there, working with him, was on the planet's surface and each of them was missing. Coollege, Stone, Hamstein, and Wilcox. Price wasn't concerned about the others from White's staff who were also missing. He was concerned that it all added up to too many people disappearing too fast.

He sat down again and scanned the most recent information, including what he could learn about Hamstein's crash. He worked through the morning, searching all the information that he had. He looked for the reasons the people might have been spotted, who they had contacted prior to leaving the ship, trying to determine who was supplying information to the enemy below. He got nowhere.

At lunchtime he decided that there was nothing more he could do on the ship. It was his job to find his missing people. He'd sent them on the assignments and now that they were gone, he had to follow up. There was no other way to look at it. And now that he had made the decision, it felt as if a weight had been lifted. Action was coming.

Coollege had felt the needle slip into her arm and the next thing she knew, she was strapped to a bed. She could move her hands slightly. She could move her feet, but the movement was restricted. Around her wrists and ankles were the soft leather of restraints. They were holding her on the cot, in a white room filled by bright sunlight.

She tugged at the restraints for a moment but they didn't slip on her wrists. As she relaxed, the door opened and the nurse appeared. She smiled down at Coollege and said, "I see you've awakened."

"Please take these straps off me," said Coollege reasonably. She was surprised by her own voice. She had wanted to demand and instead had made a request. She had been agitated and now seemed to be overly calm.

"Certainly. Just let me alert the doctor." The nurse whirled and vanished.

Coollege lay calmly, thinking that the request had been a reasonable one.

The doctor entered and asked, "How are you feeling?"

"Better."

He bent over her, examined her eyes, putting a hand on her chin and twisting her head right and left. He took her pulse and made a note of it. Finally he said, "I think we can remove those restraints." He reached down and unfastened the left one, letting it drop away.

As soon as her left hand was free, Coollege reached over

and unhooked the other. As the nurse unhooked her ankles, Coollege struggled to sit up.

When she was free, she asked, "How did I get here?"

"You don't remember?"

"The last thing I remember is leaving the spaceport this morning. Walking out of the terminal into the sun and nothing after that."

"Then you came into the spaceport this morning?" asked the doctor.

Coollege suddenly felt that she had revealed too much about herself but didn't know why. She knew that she shouldn't be talking about herself at all but her mind was muddied and it was hard to think straight.

"You came in this morning," repeated the doctor.

Since she'd already revealed that, it couldn't hurt to confirm it. She nodded and said, "But I really don't remember anything about it." Then something else appeared and she added, "I remember catching a hover car at the spaceport and riding into the downtown area."

"Where were you yesterday?" asked the doctor.

Coollege could see herself standing in the intell office on the ship, Price next to her, as they discussed all the information that was coming in. That was something that she couldn't reveal. Even thought it had to remain a secret, but she felt compelled to share it. She wanted to tell the doctor everything she could about herself. She wanted to please him, and if she had to reveal secrets, she believed she should. Yet there was something in the back of her mind telling her to remain silent.

"Do you remember yesterday?" the doctor probed gently.

"Some," she said. "Little things. Eating lunch with a friend."

"Who's the friend?"

Coollege thought about it and realized that giving the name would hurt no one. "Josh Price. We call him Tree."

"Why's that?"

"I guess it's just a nickname."

"What else do you remember?"

"Little things like that," she said.

The doctor leaned forward and examined her eyes again, shining a light into them. "There is no reason for you not to remember everything from yesterday. No reason whatsoever."

"I remember lunch."

"Where did you eat it?"

"In the cafeteria," she said. She looked down, at the restraints lying on the side of the bed.

"I'm afraid, sister, that you're not being truthful with us. You're dodging the questions when all we're trying to do is help you. Why is that?" asked the doctor.

Again she felt the urge to tell everything she knew. She wanted to please the doctor. She wanted to be one of the family that had filled Bolton's Planet, yet there was still a vestige of suspicion. Her training, years of training, told her that she should not volunteer anything to anyone at any time.

"I'm not feeling well," she said. "I would like to go to sleep."

The doctor took a deep breath and shook his head sadly. Finally he said, "Certainly. I'll have the nurse bring some medication."

Immediately she was suspicious. The last thing she wanted was additional medication. She knew of a dozen drugs that could destroy the will to resist. There were drugs that removed inhibitions, drugs that created a false sense of euphoria, drugs that depressed, and drugs that would cause her to reveal her innermost secrets. In the proper hands, such drugs could be useful tools. In other hands, they could be used to destroy a human mind.

"I would just like to get some sleep," she said.

"Of course." The doctor stood up.

"Thank you," she said.

The doctor left but a nurse returned immediately. "Doctor prescribed a sedative for you." She held the hypodermic up as if it were a trophy.

"I don't need that," said Coollege.

"Doctor's orders."

Coollege sat up, raising her hands, fingers stiff, as if facing an adversary with a knife. "I don't want a shot. I don't need a shot."

"Don't make me call for an orderly, sister. The doctor wants you to have the shot."

Coollege was going to fight it and then a feeling of calm washed over her. She felt completely relaxed. The doctor was only trying to help her. He wanted what was best for her. He wouldn't be trying to trick her. She shouldn't resist his orders or the shot. She was sure that medication was supposed to help her. She lowered her hands and then pushed up the sleeve of the gown she wore.

"Well," said the nurse, "that's more like it. Doctor will be pleased that you decided to cooperate with us. Now, this won't hurt a bit."

Coollege felt a tickling on her shoulder and then a feeling of peace and relaxation. She leaned back and closed her eyes, hoping that the doctor would visit her again in the near future.

Hamstein walked down a wide hallway filled with medical people and knocked on one of the doors. When she heard Wilcox invite her in, she entered and was surprised. She hadn't known that he had been as badly hurt as he had been. One leg was wrapped in white and stretched upward. There was a bandage on his head and both eyes were blackened. He was lying flat on his back, staring up at the ceiling, breathing shallowly and raggedly.

"How you doing?" she asked.

"Not too good, Eva. I feel rotten. Everything hurts. Everything."

"I told you to buckle your seat belt," she said, trying to be funny.

"I did," he said, not understanding. "Always have it buckled."

Hamstein found a chair and sat down. She watched as Wilcox closed his eyes and seemed to sleep for a moment. He woke with a start and looked at her. He smiled weakly.

Hamstein felt that she had to talk. "It's a good place down here."

Wilcox nodded slightly but said, "I want to go home. To the fleet. For medical help there."

"You're getting the finest care available here," said Hamstein.

"I just want to go home."

"Soon," said Hamstein. "We'll both go home soon but right now we need . . . you need to rest and recover."

Wilcox closed his eyes again. He snored once, jerked awake, and then closed his eyes again.

Hamstein stood up and watched him for a moment. She felt responsible because she had been the pilot, but she had done everything she could to get him help. Now there was nothing more she could do.

"Maybe we should just stay here forever," she said quietly, knowing that he wouldn't hear her. "Maybe that's for the best."

CHAPTER

15

Price loaded one of the small scout crafts with everything that he thought he would need on the planet's surface. That included robes and coveralls like the natives wore, a radio set to broadcast on the emergency frequency in case he needed immediate help, a weapon that could be concealed, and a small kit to carry spare shoes and sandals. He made sure that he had nothing that would identify him as an off-worlder other than the radio and weapon.

Satisfied with that, he returned to his office to check the latest intell updates. He scanned those from other intelligence officers on other ships and then read the latest assessments of what was happening on the planet's surface. The only thing he found interesting was that White had lost another two people. They'd gone off for lunch and hadn't returned. Their rooms were empty. That brought the total to five.

Price read that and asked, "What in the hell is going on down there?"

Price then sat at the keyboard, typing a complete report

into the computer. He logged it into a file that wouldn't appear on the main directory and that needed a code word to access it. If anything happened to him, someone would eventually find the file, read it, understand what had gone wrong. Price viewed it as leaving a letter with an attorney to be opened only if he was killed.

With the report done, he assessed the mainframe, flight scheduling, and inserted his own flight plan. Such documentation was to be completed by the operations officer or a member of his staff but Price, assigned under the operations umbrella, was familiar enough with the codings and flight planning that he could create his own. He was also familiar with the authorization codes, though he had no real need to know.

Finished with that, he tried to think of something else that needed to be done, but knew he was stalling. He was ready to go and there was no reason not to.

Price closed and locked his office. He walked down the long corridor, nodded at two people he recognized, and refused a lunch offer from the operations officer. He reached the shuttle bay and then entered. He walked straight to the scout ship, climbed in, and ran through the checklist quickly without turning on the battery. Satisfied that the ship was ready, he sat back and then switched on the battery and turned on the radio.

"Scout two one two, pad three, ready for launch."

"Two one two . . . is this an authorized flight?"

"Roger. Check your computer listing."

There was a moment's hesitation and then, "Roger. You're cleared. You may start engines in zero five."

"Roger, zero five." He set the clock, set the switches, and then checked the nav aids making sure that each was functioning properly. He also checked the communications equipment, sensors, and other electronic functions including radar suppression and masking capabilities. When he completed each of those, the five minutes had expired.

"I am ready to start engines," said Price.

"Two one two, you are cleared to start engines."

Price rogered and then punched a button, holding it down as the turbine began to whine. As the temperature rose, Price released the button. He touched the controls, kicking them right and left, and felt the scout ship shift on the deck.

"Two one two is ready to launch."

"Two one two, stand by."

"Roger."

The lights dimmed and the main hatch began to open. A bright yellow line on the deck showed the pathway to the hatch that Price would be required to follow.

"Two one two, you are cleared to launch."

"Roger."

Price used the directional jets to turn the ship slightly, aiming it at the open hatch. He added power a little at a time until the ship began to slide forward, the exhaust absorbed by a blast shield. As he approached the hatch, he gained speed and the instant he had cleared it, shoved the throttle to the stop, accelerating away from the main ship.

Rather than turn on a course to land on Bolton's Planet, Price entered an orbit around the system's sun. When he was more than a hundred thousand miles from the fleet, he turned again, now angling toward the interior of the system. He wasn't going to make a direct approach to Bolton's Planet. That was in case there was someone on the ship monitoring the launches of the scouts, or if the ground defense systems on the planet's surface were better than thought. A little deception went a long way.

Once he was away from the ship and had begun his trip in, he turned off everything that would produce electromagnetic radiation that might be detected from the ground. Radio signals, whether for communication or for radar, were easy to spot. His ship, with its stealth capabilities, would be a bright spot, if he used his radios and radars. To reduce the problem even more, he shut down every electrical system that he didn't need for life support and navigation.

With nothing to do as he crossed space, Price slept. The

computer navigator kept him on course and magnetometer searched for signs that another ship was approaching. The detectors would wake him if anything got too close to anything. The advantage was that the detectors searched for signals but produced none of their own.

He woke with a start, checked the instruments, and found that he was nearing the planet. There was no sign that anyone had detected him yet. He changed direction slightly and reduced his forward speed, trying to match that of the natural debris that circled the sun. He hoped that the surveillance radars below, if they somehow spotted his craft, would believe that it was nothing more than normal space debris.

He made a quick survey using the telephoto lenses of the television system and computer enhancement to search for a landing zone. Intelligence reports, gathered over the last several weeks, had uncovered and located various military and police installations. Those were plotted on the computer screen so that Price would be able to avoid them easily.

He entered a high orbit to give himself a chance to scan the ground and to search for signs that he'd been detected. Hamstein, according to the last transmissions, had been attacked while in orbit. If he spotted anyone coming toward him, he would make a run into deep space.

But there were no launches from the ground and no radar or sensors directed toward him. If they knew he was close, they were not watching him with anything he could detect. In the past, when they had found an unidentified craft, they had tried to intercept it. Since that wasn't happening, he believed that he had reached that point undetected.

"Now let's try to land," he said out loud.

He dropped the nose and entered the atmosphere, allowing the sudden resistance to bleed off some of his forward speed. As the nose began to superheat, he used the maneuvering jets to shallow the descent and to slow it. He kept the maneuvering to a minimum, using as little of the power as he could. Infrared could detect his jets, but it could also detect the heating of the ship as it passed through the atmosphere. He had to be careful that he did nothing that could be seen easily. He tried to disguise himself as a meteor or some other natural phenomena.

As he neared the ground, close to New Washington, he saw a thunderstorm with clouds that reached fifty thousand feet into air. Normally he would have avoided the storm, but this was the perfect cover for him. He dived at the cloud top, leveled off, and was immediately sucked into a downdraft. The ship dropped rapidly, nose low. Price added power, and eased into an updraft. The ship was buffeted, thrown from side to side, and then pulled down again.

Thinking that it hadn't been a good idea to fly into the clouds, Price tried to get out of the storm. He turned to the right and was shoved violently toward the ground. With his left hand, he turned on the terrain avoidance radar knowing that its signal would be lost in the constant flashes of lightning all around him.

He tried to climb, adding power, but the downdraft was too strong, pushing him toward the ground rapidly. Hail started slamming into the craft, sounding as if someone were pounding on the metal skin with a hammer. Or maybe a hundred people with a hundred hammers.

And then everything was calm. The hail was gone, the downdraft had stopped, and the winds had disappeared. He had gotten out of the main cell, but could see another two or three in front of him. It was a squall line moving slowly toward the capital city.

Price climbed again, passed between two of the towering storm cells, and put them between himself and the closest military and police base. The storm's energy would make detection difficult if not impossible.

He circled behind the storms, letting them pass over an open field, and when they were gone, he landed. He taxied close to a row of trees and then shut down the engines. When the whine of the turbine died, the only sounds were the distant rumbling of thunder and the rain pelting the side of his ship.

Price turned off the electrical equipment except for a single small light. He sat quietly, as the coolness of the ship slowly faded. He cracked the hatch letting in the humidity of the recent storm.

When the rain had slowed, Price pushed open the cockpit and climbed out. He stood in the wet grass, letting the cool breeze dry the sweat. The storms had moved off and were now over New Washington. Overhead were the last of the storm clouds breaking apart to reveal the late-afternoon sky, but more importantly, there were no military aircraft or police helicopters. Price had landed without being detected.

He turned, dragging his equipment from the interior of the ship, and then took off his flight suit. He replaced it with coveralls, put his radio and weapon, both disguised to look like innocent shaving items, into his kit, and closed the cockpit. He locked the ship, knowing that if the military or the police found it, they would drag it away.

Still satisfied that he had landed without detection, he started to walk toward New Washington. Using the standard rules of escape and evasion, Price planned to follow the worst terrain, travel at night or in bad weather, and hide during the day. He had no reason to believe that the inhabitants of Bolton's Planet were hostile, but then, too many people had dropped out of sight too quickly. Price decided to be very careful.

White's head still hurt, as if he had continued drinking through the day. He felt sick to his stomach and the thought of food made him want to run for the bathroom. He seemed to be getting sicker by the moment and while he lay on his bed, he had the urge to hold on to the sides of it.

The quiet bong at the door was a bolt of lightning through his head. He turned to look at the door but didn't have the energy to get up. He didn't even have the energy to call out so that his visitor would know he was there.

A moment later the door opened and Sister Susan stood close, asking, "Are you all right?"

"Too much to drink last night," he said, the words coming slowly and thickly.

"You look terrible," she said. "I think we'd better take you to the medicenter."

"That's not necessary. I just need to get some sleep and I'll feel better. This is the result of drinking too much."

She reached out and touched his forehead. "You're burning up. I think we'd better get you to the doctor. This isn't the result of a little too much wine."

"No," protested White. "Just let me sleep."

Sister Susan moved back to the door and then waved to someone in the hallway. Two large men in white coveralls entered. One of them crouched near White's bed and said, "Colonel let us take you to the medicenter."

"No," protested White.

"Sister," said the man, "we're going to have to take him in. Will you notify the proper people."

"Of course."

White reached up, grabbed the hand of one of the men, and said, "I will not go to the medicenter."

"Brother, you are too weak to resist us."

White let his hand drop to the bed and knew that the man was right. It made his head swim just to move and he had no strength left to fight. If they wanted to carry him out, he wouldn't be able to resist.

"Come on, brother," said the man, reaching behind White and lifting him.

"Please," protested White again.

The other man moved around, grabbed White's ankles, and swung them off the bed. "Just relax. We'll get you to the medicenter and they'll fix you right up."

White wanted to push them away. He wanted to order them to leave, but couldn't do it. He was sick to his stomach and his head was pounding. His knees buckled and he thought he was going to pass out. The room was spinning faster and faster.

"Get him into the medicenter for another treatment," said Sister Susan, ignoring White.

"Sister," warned the man.

"He won't remember this. I want him to have another treatment as quickly as possible."

"First one didn't take?"

"Some of them showed amazing resistance to the techniques. He'll come around if we're persistent."

White was aware of the discussion but it made no real sense to him. He wasn't worried about their words, but was worried about his stomach, sure that he was going to throw up at any moment.

He felt them lift him and then were carrying him through the door to be placed on a stretcher. The men lifted it and walked down the corridor. White open his eyes momentarily and saw a number of people standing there watching, concern etched on their faces. He wanted to call for help, but the words wouldn't form. He was now too weak to speak. And then he wondered why he wanted their help.

Sister Susan appeared in his field of vision, smiling down at him. "Relax, brother, and we'll have you feeling better in very short order." She took his hand, squeezing it as if to comfort him.

White wanted to shout but couldn't. Instead, he closed his eyes and fell into unconsciousness.

CHAPTER

16

Price followed the storms into New Washington, finding the streets wet from the rain and virtually deserted. Lights from the buildings created rectangles on the large green areas between them. Price avoided the light, staying on the pathways between the buildings and trying to avoid the pools of light created along them.

He found a bench and sat down. He stared up at one of the residence buildings and wondered what was happening inside it. That was something that he would have to find out soon. There were a dozen, a hundred things that came to mind now that he was in the capital. He wished that he'd thought of them before he left.

Finally he stood and walked toward the closest of the buildings. As he approached the door, a man standing just inside, apparently watching the last of the storm as it drifted away, waved at him. Price waved back and walked in.

"Welcome, brother," said the man. "Are you just arriving?"

"Just a few minutes ago. From the spaceport."

"What section are you assigned to?"

Price had no idea what the correct answer was supposed to be. He didn't know if a number was required or an occupation or maybe just a name. "I'm going to be a botanist," he said cautiously.

"Then you're in the wrong building. You need to be down two from here. Botanists are housed there."

Price smiled and said, "Why thank you, brother. The driver was a little confused."

"Happens sometimes," said the man. "Would you like me to show you the way?"

"If it wouldn't be too much trouble."

"Not at all. I remember what it was like when I first arrived. New Washington is so large that it is confusing if you're not used to it."

"And all the buildings look exactly the same."

"Of course."

They walked out a side door and along a walkway. A woman hurried toward them, head down, but she looked up, smiled, and said, "Good evening, brothers."

"Good evening, sister."

They passed between two large buildings. "That is the largest residence hall in the city. More than four thousand people live in it. Think of it. Four thousand people living under one roof. And that, over there, is the medicenter. That's very handy for us here."

"I imagine," said Price.

"Right there is the residence hall for you."

"Thank you, brother," said Price. "You've been very kind."

"Good luck, brother."

Price walked toward the residence hall and entered it. There were a number of people sitting in the atrium area talking. One of them looked up and waved but didn't stand. Price walked past them and stepped on the escalator. No one seemed concerned that he was there or that none of them had seen him before.

"New here, brother?" asked a voice behind him.

Price turned and said, "Just arrived today. Assigned to botany."

"I'll alert the house leader for you."

"Thank you," said Price. He watched as the man hurried off. Price didn't know if he should try to get out now, before anyone could ask for orders or check with the computer, or if he should just ride it out.

But the house leader appeared before Price could make up his mind. He came forward and said, "Welcome, brother. My name is Pete."

"John," said Price. He figured that there was a good chance that many people were named John. Joshua might be pushing it a little.

"I didn't know that we were going to get some help in here," said Pete.

"Well, I'm glad to be here," said Price.

"Have you been to the medicenter?"

"Not yet. I just arrived a few minutes ago. I wanted to get settled in first."

"We'll get you scheduled in the morning, brother. Where did you come from?"

Price hesitated, unsure of how to answer.

"Just out of school?" prompted the house leader.

"Yes," said Price. "Just graduated. This is my first assignment away from the school."

"Well, I'm sure that you'll enjoy botany. I know we're not supposed to say anything, but I think this is the best of assignments. We have the opportunity to do so much for the planet." He clapped Price on the shoulder. "I know. It's sacrilege to talk this way, but you'll see once you get started. We're all so lucky."

"I always thought that," said Price cautiously, "but I was afraid to say it out loud."

Pete smiled knowingly. "Let's see, I think there is an empty cube up on four. The brother there became ill and was transferred to a warmer climate for his health. That's the thing around here. We're always thinking of each other. Help our brothers and sisters.''

They walked to an escalator and took it up. They got off on four and moved to a door. Pete reached down, turned the knob, and pushed. ''I'm afraid that it doesn't have a window, but the new brother can't expect to have a window first thing. You have to be patient.''

''It doesn't matter, really. At least I'm not sharing it with another and that's the first time I've had a room to myself,'' said Price.

''Sharing? I didn't know they were doubling up at the school.''

''Ah, well, one hall was damaged by fire and we had to share for a month.''

Pete didn't catch the contradiction. ''Oh. Of course. Have you eaten yet?''

''Not since this morning.''

''Well, drop your kit on the cot and we'll go down to the cafeteria.''

Price set it on the cot and turned. ''Let's go.''

They rode the escalator down to the ground level and walked into the cafeteria. There wasn't much of a selection. Just a processed loaf, some bread, and tea.

''Should have been here for dinner,'' said Pete. ''It was extra good tonight.'' He laughed. ''I know that I'm going to begin to sound like a cheerleader, but I think we've got the best cafeteria staff here. Food is always excellent. You were very lucky to be assigned here.''

Price made a sandwich, filled a cup with tea, and set it on the closest table. ''Is the cafeteria open all night?''

''Why would it be?'' asked Pete.

''I thought we might have to run all-night shifts here. Some areas are doing that.''

''Nope,'' said Pete. ''Two shifts with everyone back and asleep by midnight.''

Price took a bite from his sandwich and tried to think of how to ask his questions. He needed to try to find some of the missing people, but didn't know how to ask. Since he was claiming to have just entered the city, he wouldn't know what had happened the day before. But he needed a clue so that he could begin his search.

"What's it like," he asked finally, "living here in the capital?"

"It's the most exciting city. Everything is focused here. Visitors from the outer planets are often seen on the streets as they sightsee here. You're lucky to have been assigned here."

"Isn't there a delegation from Earth here now?"

"You've heard about that?" asked Pete.

"Well, I don't live in a cave," said Price. "We do hear some things."

"Of course. There has been some trouble with them. Some of them have gotten sick. They've spent their time in the medicenter."

"That's too bad," said Price. "So much to do and then have to stay in the medicenter."

"Well, I guess spaceflight and then being on a strange planet can cause you some trouble. But I understand that most of them have recovered."

"Where are they staying?"

Pete smiled broadly. "Going to look at the aliens?"

"No . . ."

"Well, there's not much to see anyway. They look just like us. A little rough around the edges but they're human."

"Of course they are," said Price. "Still, I haven't seen anyone from Earth."

Pete stood up and said, "It's getting close to lights out. I'll let you finish here and then you'd better get settled. I'll be back in the morning and we'll go over to the medicenter and get you set there."

"Thank you, Pete. You've been very kind."

"Don't mention it." Pete walked to the door, turned and waved, and then disappeared.

Price finished his sandwich and then studied the cafeteria.

Plenty of food available and it apparently worked on the same system as a military mess hall. Food was prepared and those who were hungry came to eat it. Everyone got his or her fill and then left. If he wanted, Price figured he could fill his kit with food. Enough for several days.

Of course, there didn't seem to be any accounting system. He could enter any cafeteria anywhere in the city and get something to eat. That certainly solved one of the problems.

A feminine voice came over a speaker announcing, "Lights must be turned out in ten minutes. Lights must be turned out in ten minutes."

Price finished his meal, took the plate and glass to a small window, and then went back to his room. He unrolled the cot and laid down on it. He heard the woman announce that there were five minutes, then one minute, and finally that lights should be out.

"Have a good night," she said.

The lights went out. Price sat up but didn't stand. He listened to the activities in the building. There were a few people moving around. Price wondered if the men and women waited for lights out as they did on the ship, and then joined one another figuring that no one knew what was happening. He wondered if he looked out the door if he would see a half-dozen people trying to slip into the rooms of their friends and lovers.

Patience, he told himself, was the key to success. Those who ran out of patience often found themselves failing in their missions. Price would be patient. He would wait for the people to settle down and go to sleep. Then he would sneak out and walk over to the medicenter.

When Price opened his door after waiting several hours, the hallway was dark and empty. He walked out and no bells went off, no buzzers sounded, and no police jumped out to arrest him. Price walked to the escalator, which had been shut down. No sense in using power for it when there wouldn't be much demand for it. Price walked down.

The door was open when he got there. The humidity of the evening was gone. It was cool outside, almost pleasant. Price walked out the door and headed toward the medicenter. No one challenged him. The whole area was deserted. No one was out at that time.

The medicenter was nearly as deserted. A nurse sat behind a desk and looked up as he entered but when he said nothing to her, she bent back to her work. That surprised Price but it also pleased him. In a society where no one was suspicious of anyone, he could move around easily.

He took the escalator to the second floor and walked down it slowly. Most of the wide doors were open and he could see into the rooms. Some of the people looked as if they were very sick or badly injured. Stacks of equipment monitored their vital signs. Others seemed to be well, in rooms with nothing other than a bed, a chair, and a nightstand.

He stopped in one doorway and stared at the person in the bed. He didn't recognize her but then there was no reason to believe that he would. He then moved on to the next room, saw a man sitting up and staring at the door. Price didn't recognize him either.

He continued down the hall and found no one he knew. He didn't know why he thought he'd find someone he knew there, but he continued the search.

When he reached the end, he found a stairway, and climbed to the next floor. It was a carbon copy of the floor below. Near the middle by the escalator was a light marking the nurse's station but there was no one there. Price pushed the door all the way open and walked out into the hallway. As he started down it, searching, he heard a voice call out from one of the rooms, "Captain Price?"

Price froze in his tracks, trying to place the voice. He turned and looked into the room. Hamstein was sitting on the edge of her bed looking straight at him.

"What are you doing here?" Hamstein asked.

"I could ask you the same thing."

"I . . ." She shrugged. "I crashed my ship and was brought here."

"Any of the others here?"

"Wilcox is here. He was hurt pretty bad. He's the only one I've seen."

"You okay?"

"Yes, sir. Banged up a little but mostly I'm just tired. I've been resting."

"You ready to get the hell out of here then?"

She looked at him and said, "I'd better stay."

"Why?"

"I just think I should. For a day or so. Maybe I'll feel different in the morning."

Price studied her for a moment and then said, "Whatever you think is best . . . You won't mention to anyone that you saw me, will you?"

"No, sir," she said. "No. I won't mention it."

"Okay," said Price. "See you later." He moved away from the door, suddenly concerned that Hamstein was going to tell. He didn't know why, but that was the impression he had.

CHAPTER

17

After speaking with Hamstein, Price decided that it was time to get out because he'd pressed his luck about as far as it would go. He didn't want to get trapped on the third floor of the medicenter when someone raised the alarm. If someone raised the alarm. He ran down the stairs, stopped on the landings and listened, and then hurried out along the ground floor. No one in the medicenter seemed to care that he was there or that he was leaving.

As he opened the door to leave, he noticed a flash of light. He dropped back and pushed the door closed. He tried to visualize what he had just seen. A searchlight on a helicopter? He'd seen no sign of the chopper and he'd heard nothing that sounded like a helicopter but that didn't mean much.

He pushed himself away from the door and climbed the stairs again. He found a room where the patient was asleep and walked to the window. Looking out he spotted some movement along one of the walkways in front of the medicenter but that meant nothing by itself. He crouched on

the floor and looked up, toward the sky. The black shape of
a helicopter hovered about two hundred feet above the
ground, the sound of the engine and rotor masked.

"Shit."

He shifted around and looked down at the walkway. Now
everything below him was sinister. All movement was from
the police slipping into position to capture him. All bushes
concealed officers waiting to trap him.

He dropped to the floor, sitting with his back to the wall,
his knees drawn up, and his head bowed so that it wouldn't
be visible from below. "How in the hell did they find me?"

The shape in the bed stirred, mumbled something, and
then slipped back into sleep.

Price crawled away from the window and then stood up.
He had to get out of the medicenter. That was as far as his
thinking took him. Just get the hell out. Once outside, he
would have room to maneuver.

He stepped to the door, and looked out but there was no
one in the hallway. It was as quiet as a tomb and as deserted
as the moon. He exited and moved to the right, to the stairs
there. He ran up, toward the top floor, knowing that he
should be going down. The simple rule was to never get
away from the ground floor if it could be helped.

He came out on the fifth floor and worked his way along
it. He tried various doors, searching for something that
would help him. He'd thought about locking himself in a
room but the police would be able to get the key. A
thorough search would require the police to check every
room. He needed something that would help him get out of
the medicenter.

Failing on the fifth floor, he used the escalator to the top
floor and finally headed for the roof. He opened the door
and looked out at the flat top of the building. He spotted
nothing that could help him get back down to the ground,
but he exited anyway, wanting to get another view of the
police operation below him.

The chopper had landed in front of the medicenter. A ring

of police, difficult to see because of their black uniforms, were near the entrance to the medicenter. It appeared that police had been sent to watch each of the other exits, keeping Price bottled up in the building.

Crouching at the edge of the roof, looking down, it was apparent there was no easy way to escape. There were places where only one officer was on guard, but Price didn't want to attack there. He wanted to slip away, into the night with no one the wiser, if that was possible. He wanted to do nothing to further antagonize the police.

No one below seemed to be in a rush. They were sealing the area so that he couldn't escape. They were going at it in a methodical, professional fashion. It was obvious that they knew what they were doing.

Price rubbed his chin and wiped his hand through his hair. He thought of Hamstein, on the second floor of the medicenter, and decided that he'd better get her out of there while he had the chance. She might be able to provide him with additional information. She'd been in the medicenter for several hours and might have seen something.

He hurried back to the second floor and found Hamstein standing at the window watching as the police began to search the medicenter. She wore a short, white hospital gown that was completely open in the rear.

"They're looking for you," she said without turning to look at him.

"I figured as much. You turn me in?"

"I'm sorry, Tree, but it's for your own good. They'll get you fixed right up."

"There is nothing wrong with me," said Price. "Nothing at all."

She turned away from the window. "They'll help you understand the society here. It's not hostile or dangerous. They've solved so many of humanity's problems and all they want is to help the rest of us understand."

"Let's you and me get out of here."

"Why?"

"Come on, Eva, we don't have time. They're looking for me. One man by myself. You can help me walk out the door."

"That won't fool them," she said. "Besides, I'm staying here."

"I don't want to make this an order but I do outrank you," he said.

"Yes," she said slowly, "but we have an obligation to obey a higher authority if the question is a moral one."

"No morality here," said Price. "I just want you to go with me so that I can get out of here."

"But they're coming to help you," she said. "You need their help."

"Maybe. Maybe not. But at the moment the choice is mine and I don't want to be around for it. I want to get out of here. That's all."

"No."

"Lieutenant, it isn't a request. Besides, no one will get hurt."

Hamstein was quiet for a moment and then said, "All right. I'll help you get out of here, but once you're clear, I'm coming back."

"Fine. Get dressed."

Hamstein walked to the closet and took out the flight suit she had been wearing when picked up. She pulled off the medicenter gown and tossed it on the bed.

Price had been watching the police through the window. They were beginning to advance on the doors. Time was running out. He glanced at Hamstein. "No. Not a flight suit. We've got to get you some local clothes."

"These are all I have."

Price moved to the closet and yanked the door wide. White coveralls hung in the rear. He pulled them from the hook and tossed them to Hamstein. "Wear these."

When she was dressed, Price walked to the door, glanced at the hallway, and found it still vacant. "Okay," he said, "we walk out of here and through the police line. We tell them that you had been feeling ill and we came here for medical assistance. Now we're going back to our residence.''

''They'll never believe that.''

Price took a deep breath and knew that she was right. His only hope was that they were searching for a single male and might overlook a couple. He doubted that but there was nothing else to do except hide with the very real possibility that the police would find him quickly.

Together they walked to the central escalator. They rode it to the ground floor and spotted two of the black-clad police officers standing near the exit. Another was consulting with a nurse and a doctor.

Price felt a chill on his spine, as if one of the officers were aiming his weapon at his back. Price ignored the feeling and turned his attention to Hamstein. ''You look much better now than you did when we came in.''

''I feel better too,'' she said, but she didn't sound convincing.

One of the police officers looked at them, nodded, but made no move toward them. Price nodded back, smiled, and said, ''Brother.''

They walked out the door and toward the chopper that was sitting on the ground, the rotors whirling. Price tried to keep his eyes off the police and the helicopter, not wanting to draw attention to himself.

They drew even with the chopper when one of the police officers called, ''What are the two of you doing out here at this time?''

''She was feeling ill,'' said Price. ''We came over here for some medication.''

Hamstein remained quiet for a moment and then said, ''But I feel better now.''

''You should be asleep,'' said the officer.

''Certainly, sister,'' said Price. ''It was an unusual circumstance.'' He was going to add more but knew that was the mistake of the amateur. Fill the air with the sound of his own voice, adding detail that wasn't required.

The officer left her post and walked over to Price. She glanced at him and said, "You're new around here."

"Yes. I was just assigned."

"Where?"

"Botany," said Price. He pointed to one of the buildings. "Residence hall over there."

The cop pushed up the silver visor on her helmet revealing a face that looked to be twelve years old. "You got a pass from your house leader."

"No," said Hamstein.

"We just walked over here. I didn't think that we'd need to bother anyone else."

"Should have gotten a pass," said the cop.

"Of course," said Price. He was about to walk away and then thought better of it. Since the police had stopped him, now was the time to ask questions. He hitchhiked a thumb over his shoulder and asked, "What's happening?"

"Sick man in the medicenter." She thought about how that sounded and then laughed. "I mean, someone who is mentally ill rather than physically."

"I hope that you find him and help him, sister."

"Don't worry. We know he's in there now. It's just a question of carefully searching each and every floor until we locate him."

"Well, good luck."

"Thank you."

Price tugged at Hamstein and began to walk toward his residence hall. He kept waiting for a voice to shout for him to stop, but it never came.

As they left the area, Hamstein said, "I don't believe it. We walked right past them and no one questioned a thing."

"They're looking for one man, not a couple." Price couldn't keep the surprise out of his voice.

"You're clear. You can let me return to the hospital now," said Hamstein.

"Why?" asked Price. "You weren't hurt in the crash and you look fine to me."

"I just want to go back. I have to go back. My treatment hasn't been completed."

"Treatment?" said Price.

"Medication," she said. "To help me out. I need to get back for it."

They reached the residence hall and entered it. Price led her up to his room and then shut the door once they were inside. The tiny red light came on so that they could see. Price sat on the floor. Hamstein sat on the cot, tucking her feet up under her.

Price was listening, waiting for someone to come after him. When the police failed to find him in the medicenter, they would be on their way to his residence hall. He was the only one to leave the medicenter and he had told the police officer where he was going.

"You know," said Hamstein. "They have all the answers."

Price didn't understand what she meant but said, "I've heard that. I don't believe it, but I've heard it. They sure convinced you quickly."

"It's just a matter of opening my eyes and seeing the truth," said Hamstein. She ran a hand through her hair, fanning it out. She shook her head once. "I can see the difference between the people here and all those I know. Their system is the better."

"Sure."

"Look at it . . ."

"Eva, I'm not interested in your assessment of the society here at the moment. I'm more concerned with all the missing people from the landing team."

"What missing people."

Price stood up and put an ear against the door. It was still quiet outside. He wished that he had a window so that he could see what was happening outside.

"Our missing people. Rocky, Jackknife, and about half of the landing team."

"They're not missing," said Hamstein calmly. "They're at the medicenter."

"What?"

"They're at the medicenter. Some of them have been very sick. They're being treated. I've seen them there."

Price focused his attention on her. "Treated? What do you mean they're being treated?"

"Like me. Medication to take care of their problems." She shrugged. "Treatments."

Price began to understand then. It was suddenly obvious how so many people had been picked up so fast. Hamstein didn't seem to understand the concept of military secrecy anymore. She was sharing information as if it was the natural thing to do. The instant she had the chance, she'd alerted the police about him. She was more open and honest than Price had ever seen her.

"What is this medication?" he asked.

"Nothing much. Just to help us fight any disease that we might contract on the planet. Things like that. Maybe a little tranquilizer to help us relax. We need about two weeks of medication before we're allowed to return to the mainstream. Now, I really should get back to the medicenter. They're going to be worried."

"I think we'd better return to the ship."

Hamstein smiled. "Not yet. I'm not ready. I helped you because you needed it, but I really have to return. I don't want to miss tomorrow's treatment."

"You're staying with me and we're getting the hell out of here," said Price.

"Let me get my treatment in the morning and then I'll return with you. I really need it."

"No," said Price. He looked at her as if she were a drug addict. She wanted her treatment in the same way that a user wanted his next fix. "What have they done to you?"

"You don't understand. These treatments help us. I feel much better now."

"You're going to stay right here," said Price, "and the first chance we get, we're going back to the fleet."

Hamstein stood up and said, "There isn't anything you can do to stop me. I'm going back to the medicenter."

Price centered himself on the door and shook his head. "We're both staying here for the rest of the night and then getting out. Those are your orders."

"I won't tell you're here; I just want to get my treatment. That's all."

"Settle down," said Price. He cocked his head and put his ear against the door. "They're coming now. Quiet."

"Let me go to them. I'll tell them you've escaped."

Price shook his head again. "No. We'll go together and we'll make it together, or we'll both be caught."

Hamstein smiled broadly. "Whatever you say, Captain."

CHAPTER

18

All the lights in the building had been turned on. The public-address system was asking that everyone step out into the hallway. That was all. Just step into the hallway until the police passed and then return to the room. It was all made to sound very routine.

"There is no way for you to escape," said Hamstein, sounding pleased.

"There is always a way to escape. I just have to be clever enough to figure it out."

"You can't make it with me," said Hamstein. "I'll slow you down."

Price studied her for a moment and thought that if he couldn't make it out with her, then he'd have to kill her. In her current state, she was a threat to him and to his mission. She would tell everything that she knew as quickly as she could in her misguided attempt to help him and that would sabotage any follow-up plans that Price might have.

"But I can help you," she said. "Just let me surrender to

the police. I'll tell them you're gone and then I can get my treatment in the morning."

"Shut up and let me think," said Price.

"You're stuck if you don't let me help."

Price ignored that. Sudden violence, sudden unexpected violence, often provided an opening. If he attacked and then ran, he might be able to get clear. If he could get out of the building, his chances improved. If he attacked one or two police officers in the stairwell, he might be able to get out of the building before anyone realized what he had done. All other courses had been sealed now.

The problem was Hamstein. She would not cooperate. She would do everything she could to slow him down and expose him to the enemy. The smart course was to kill her in the room, hide the body, and get out before it was discovered. That was the smart thing.

"You're coming with me," said Price. "I don't want any trouble from you."

"Just leave me here."

"The debate is over," said Price. "We're getting out of here."

"Yes, sir."

Price opened the door and found that everyone else on the floor was already in the hall. They were standing next to their doors almost as if waiting for an inspection from a higher-ranking officer.

Lowering his voice, he said, "We're going to avoid the escalator, use the fire stairs, and then head for the outskirts of the city."

"This is unnecessary."

"Just do it and you won't get hurt."

"Yes, sir."

"Come on." Price exited, nodded to the man standing across the hall, and then, with Hamstein in tow, walked to the far end. The people watched him but not one of them said a word to them or tried to raise the alarm.

Price opened the door and started down the steps with

Hamstein right behind him. He stopped and held up a hand when he heard someone on the stairs below him.

To Hamstein, he said, ''I'm counting on you to help me here. We're fellow officers.''

She didn't respond.

Price started down again and at the landing found a police officer.

''Sorry, brother, but you must return to your room.''

Price didn't say a word. He walked up to the officer, grabbed the front of his uniform, and jerked him forward. He used a knee and when the man began to fall, clipped him on the back of the neck. The officer dropped with a sigh and didn't move. Price knelt and searched for a pulse.

''You kill him?''

''Nope. Heart's beating away. He'll be fine in a little while.''

They reached the ground floor and Price pushed open the door. Another police officer caught it and looked right at him. ''What are you doing here?''

''The officer upstairs is ill. He asked me to have you take his place.''

''He knows better than that. I can't leave this post without permission.''

''I was afraid you'd say that.'' Price's hand shot out, punching at the chest of the police officer. As he staggered back, Price grabbed his shirt, twisted his hip into the officer's belly, and flipped him to the ground. He grabbed at the weapon the man dropped.

''Halt!''

''Run,'' yelled Price but Hamstein stood as if rooted to the spot.

One of the police officers fired, the beam flashing over Price's head. Price shot back, aiming at a bench. It exploded, the wood flaring.

The officer dived to the right, rolled to his belly, and shot again. The beam struck the ground with an audible pop, the grass baking and the soil boiling.

"Run!" ordered Price.

Hamstein hesitated a second longer and then whirled. She sprinted down the walkway, hurtled a bench, and crouched behind it.

Price stood up and fired his weapon as if it were a fire hose. He sprayed the area, destroying a light post, another bench, and two bushes. Bits of flaming debris erupted and scattered. With the police scrambling for cover, he ran toward Hamstein.

"Follow me," he said as he ran past her.

Without a thought, Hamstein was up and running. She caught up with Price and stayed with him. A lamppost near them exploded, the flaming debris raining down.

"That way," said Price. He turned toward a building and ran for the door.

Two police officers appeared on the right, angling toward them. Price squeezed off a shot, the beam lancing out. The officers turned, running for cover.

The helicopter launched itself, leaping straight up. The nose dipped as it turned toward them. Price saw it out of the corner of his eye, but ignored it.

They reached the door of the building and ran through. Hamstein stopped at the foot of the escalator, bent at the waist, breathing hard.

"We have . . . to . . . surrender."

Price wondered about that. With the helicopter in the air, there seemed little chance for them to escape. There wasn't the cover necessary for them to lose the aircraft. It could hover above them, outside the range of the weapons, and watch every move they made, directing the police toward them easily.

Price ran forward, grabbed Hamstein's hand, and said, "Come on. Out the back."

"Won't do any good."

He was afraid that she was right, but wasn't going to give up easily. He dragged her around the escalator and down the hallway. They came to another exit and Price pushed it open slowly, searching the area outside quickly. It looked as if it was clear.

He slipped out, pulling Hamstein with him. He could hear the police attempting to surround the building. They were cautious, afraid of the weapon he held.

Together, Price and Hamstein slipped along the side of the building. They rounded a corner and Price jerked her forward. They ran across the open courtyard, straight at the entrance of another residence hall. Price ran through it, down the hallway, and out the back of it, dragging Hamstein with him.

In front of them was another building, but this one was brightly lighted. That scared Price, so he turned, aiming at another residence hall. They ran through it as they had the last and once they were back outside, Price slid to a stop.

"We lost them for the moment."

Hamstein fell back, against the smooth stone of the building, and sucked at the air. "They'll find us."

Price slipped to one knee and then surveyed the area. There was row after row of buildings, all precisely placed and built giving the city a uniform look. It was a grid that had been carefully planned before the first structure had been erected.

He wiped at the sweat on his forehead that threatened to drip into his eyes. He glanced up and saw that the sky was beginning to brighten. He knew that he had to find a good hiding place before the sun came up. There was no way he could avoid capture in the daylight.

"Let me go," said Hamstein suddenly. "I'm just slowing you down."

"We get out of this together or we don't."

"You're being foolish."

"Maybe," said Price.

The chopper appeared overhead, a spotlight shining down. It circled the building. Price jumped up, flattening himself against the side. The helicopter hovered for an instant and then slipped off, playing its bright light over the courtyard between the buildings.

"They're looking for someone running," said Price.

"They'll be back."

"Come on," said Price. He pulled her along the side of the building. They came to the edge and Price stopped. There was no one moving out there. The police had circled one of the buildings they had run through. The chopper was off to the south, searching for them.

"We're going to run to that building over there. We're going to head straight for the door. You got that?"

"Yes."

"Okay." Price surveyed the area again and then said, "On three."

"I'm staying here."

"We go on three," said Price. "One, two, three." He pushed her in the back and she stumbled forward, but then began to run. Price was right behind her.

They crossed the open area quickly and ran through the open door, but the ground floor wasn't empty. A police officer stood near the escalator. She was dressed in riot gear including a black helmet with a silver faceplate on it.

"Stop!" She began to lift her radio to her lips so that she could alert the rest of the search team.

Price fired, hitting her in the hand. The radio dropped to the floor and broke. She dived to her left and fired once. The beam struck Hamstein in the chest. Without a word, Hamstein sat down and then rolled to her side.

Price shot again and the officer fell onto the escalator. As the body began to ascend, Price crouched next to Hamstein. He touched her throat, searching for a pulse but found nothing. The smoking hole in her chest was big enough for a fist. Price knew it killed her.

But that could be the chance he needed. He stood up and then ran to the escalator. The police officer's body was at the top, jammed up against the railing.

He thought about calling for help but decided that he

could use the few minutes of lead time. Let the police try to figure it out while he was getting out of the area.

He ran toward the back of the building, threw open the door, and ran out. Overhead he heard the quiet pop of the rotor blades and knew that he had made a mistake. The spotlight came on, pinning him in the center of it. Price stopped and stood still, staring at the helicopter as it descended slowly, landing fifty feet away from him.

Two police officers jumped out. One of them hung back but the other walked forward slowly. The pilot opened his door and put a foot up on the side of the helicopter, relaxing.

"Brother," said the police officer, "what are you doing out so early?"

"Help. We need help. An officer has been injured . . ."

"Did you tell the house leader?"

"I was . . . there's a police officer down." Price pointed at the residence hall.

"You wait right here. Don't move."

"Certainly, brother."

The police officer ran toward the door and disappeared into the interior of the building. As he did, Price walked toward the chopper.

"It was terrible," he said. "Just terrible. They shot the police officer. Killed her."

The officer near the helicopter used his radio, his voice quiet, impossible for Price to understand. Then he said to Price, "You wait here, by the chopper."

"Of course, brother."

As the second officer ran toward the building, Price walked slowly toward the cockpit of the helicopter. Only the pilot remained inside.

As he approached, Price asked, "What's going on?"

The pilot looked down at Price as if he didn't deserve an answer but then said, "Searching for a sick brother and sister. They ran out of the medicenter."

"Near here?"

"Over that way," said the pilot, pointing to the north.

Getting closer, Price asked, "Is it difficult to fly one of these?"

The pilot didn't answer for a moment and then nodded. "Not at all," he said, warming to the topic. "Not once you get the hang of it. It's harder to learn than an airplane but I think anyone can learn the skill if they take enough time."

Price walked closer as if he wanted to see into the cockpit but grabbed the front of the pilot's shirt instead, jerking at it. The pilot slapped at his hands, his seat belt and shoulder harness holding him in place.

"What in the hell are you doing?"

Price twisted around, punched at the man's chest, and then grabbed at the seat belt. He jerked it open and yanked at the pilot. Now he fell forward. His right hand shot out, to brace himself on the instrument panel. Price slammed a hand into the pilot's elbow. He roared in sudden pain. Price twisted and pulled and the pilot came up, out of his seat. He fell facedown to the ground, and Price struck at the back of the neck, knocking out the pilot.

He stepped over the body, climbed into the seat, and scanned the instrument panel quickly. He reached for the collective and then rolled on the throttle, increasing the speed of the rotor. The whine of the turbine turned to a howl. Price touched the pedals, and then with one hand on the cyclic and the other on the collective tried to pick up to a hover. The aircraft broke ground and leapt twenty feet into the air. Price fought the controls, using the cyclic and the pedals to stabilize the movement. Satisfied, he used the pedals to turn ninety degrees to the right. The area in front of him was clear.

He pushed forward on the cyclic, pulling in a little collective as he did. The nose of the chopper fell as he began to pick up forward speed. He grinned to himself as he pulled back on the stick and then added power with the throttle and collective to begin a rapid climb. In seconds he was a couple of hundred feet above the buildings, racing to the west, where he had stashed his ship.

The radio crackled to life. "Chopper three, say status."

Price spotted the radio control but didn't touch it. There was nothing that he wanted to say and there was no way he could answer the question.

"Chopper three, please say status."

In answer, Price descended until he was only a few feet above the buildings. He skimmed over the tops of them, dodging right and left, trying to stay as low as possible. In the distance he could see the edge of the city. Not far beyond that was the safety of his ship.

He glanced over his shoulders but there was no one in pursuit. He'd caught them by surprise. In ten minutes he would be clear. He'd be out of the city.

Behind him the sky was beginning to brighten rapidly. The ground, locked in shifting shadows turned from black to charcoal to gray. He could make out the bushes and trees of the greenbelts. Lights on the walkways began to flicker and die. Morning was coming to the city.

And then he was over the last of the buildings and descending so that he was only a few feet above the ground. He jumped over tree lines and bushes and chased two people from a pathway. As they dived into the ditches to avoid being hit, he laughed at them.

He slowed after a few minutes and then stopped, pulling back on the collective to hover fifty feet in the air. He scanned the ground around him, slid off to the right, and stopped again. Below him, hidden close to the trees, right where he left it, was his ship. No one had discovered it, no one had disturbed it, and it looked as if no one was guarding it.

He lowered the collective, worked at the pedals, and slowly settled to the ground. As soon as he touched down, he pushed the collective to the lower stop and rolled back the throttle. He reached up to shut off the main fuel switch and as the turbine unwound, he flipped the battery switch to the off position. In seconds it was quiet in the field. No sound from anywhere. No sign of pursuit.

Price climbed from the chopper, patted the side as if to thank it for the lift, and then walked to his ship. He opened the cockpit and climbed in, checking it quickly. There was no sign that anyone had tampered with it. Within five minutes, he was ready to take off. The enemy didn't show, police choppers didn't fill the air above him, and no one surrounded him.

As soon as his ship was ready, the turbine at full RPM, the instruments, radars, and sensors scanning the fields and skies around him, he rolled out, away from both the chopper and the trees that had concealed him. He accelerated over the flat, smooth field, using it like a runway on an old-fashioned airport, reached transition, and pulled back on the yoke. Flying like an airplane in an atmosphere, he gained altitude rapidly. He scanned his instruments repeatedly, but there was no indication that anyone was tracking him. His getaway had been clean.

At one hundred thousand feet, he engaged the rocket engines that propelled him into the upper reaches of the atmosphere. As he entered the blackness of space, he knew that he had made it. No one from Bolton's Planet would be able to catch him now.

CHAPTER

19

White was sitting in his bed in the medicenter, eating his breakfast that consisted of soft foods cooked to a consistency of soggy cardboard, but he wasn't complaining. The headache was gone and his stomach had settled. The idea of eating appealed to him even if the food was gray, soggy and tasteless. At least it was hot and filling and at the moment that was all he cared about.

Sister Susan sat in the visitor's chair watching him shovel the food into his mouth. She smiled at him and said, "You seem to feel better today."

He put his spoon down and nodded. "Much better. I don't know why I was so insistent that I be allowed to remain in my room. Just stupid."

"We had the same trouble with a number of your staff," said Sister Susan.

Puzzled by that, White asked, "How many of them are here now?"

"Twelve of them. We don't know what happened but it seems that everyone who attended the reception became ill.

No, that's not quite right. It was only the people in your party. We have our scientists looking into it but believe there must have been something in the food to which we're immune but that you, as off-worlders, are not. That has to be what caused the problem. It's the only thing we can think of.''

"Very strange," said White.

"We'll get an answer soon," said Sister Susan.

"I'm sure you will." White picked up his spoon and finished his breakfast. He then drank his juice. Holding up the glass, he asked, "What is this?"

"Native plant that's not unlike the orange. A little tangier and a little larger, but filled with vitamin C."

"I've noticed that many things on his planet are a little better than similar things on Earth," said White.

"We have tried to make our society a little better than those that have gone before it. I think that we have succeeded in that."

"I agree," said White. "In fact, I plan to petition for a release from active service so that I might join you here. This is what I've been looking for since I first left Earth so many years ago."

"I'm delighted to hear that," said Sister Susan. "But maybe you should look to returning here on retirement. You have an opportunity to spread the word about us. And how would you feel about deserting your career?"

"I don't believe I would be deserting anything," said White. "Still, once you've found your true home, why leave it? I see this as my home."

"True." She stood up and stepped to the bed. "Are you willing to speak with members of your staff today?"

"About what?"

"A few have been resisting our treatment. They have the unreasonable belief that we're trying to trick them in some fashion. They want to return to the fleet before they take any treatment."

"There are always those who want to create trouble,"

said White. "After breakfast, I'll talk to them. I'm sure that we can settle this problem easily and quickly. I mean, I felt the same way yesterday."

"Yes, you did."

Price wasn't interested in finesse this time. He wasn't trying to disguise his flight route. He wanted to get back to his ship as quickly as he could, before the enemy could launch any kind of intercept. He had to report because he understood what was happening on Bolton's Planet. Understood it completely and totally and hoped that he could convince the Colonel that he was right about it.

Once he had cleared the planet's orbit and was accelerating toward the fleet, he began to relax. Now that he was racing away from the planet, he turned on every sensor, radar, and detector on board. He let them scan space all around him, searching for electromagnetic radiation, for radar, for infrared. If anything was near him, he wanted to know about it. Nothing would get close without him seeing it and preparing to engage it.

With that set up and the ship on autopilot, he had a moment to relax. He closed his eyes, and when he did, he saw Hamstein lying on the floor, the gaping, bloody hole in her chest. He could hear her protesting his orders, wanting to stay in the medicenter. If he'd done what she wanted, she would still be alive.

But that thought was overpowered by what he had learned from her and the fact that she had turned him in to the authorities. If he'd left her in the room, she probably would have helped them apprehend him, telling them everything they would need to catch him. The only course of action was to take her with him. He'd been right about that. If she had cooperated, she would still be alive. Her death was her own fault.

He woke with a start an hour later. His scout craft was now approaching the fleet. He turned the IFF so they would know that he was friendly.

The radio crackled to life a moment later. "Incoming craft, please say ID."

"Scout two one two. Launched yesterday and returning to base."

"Roger." There was a hesitation and then, "You are cleared to approach. Please call at one thousand klicks."

"Roger."

When he was a thousand klicks away, he made his call and was cleared on in. He worked his way through the outer screen of ships, the smaller vessels set up to defend against attack from space in much the same fashion that destroyers had once protected aircraft carriers in Earth's surface fleets. He knew that each of the screening vessels was watching him closely in case he suddenly changed course. They wanted to be in a position to attack him if needed.

He turned his scout craft, aiming at the center of the fleet. He picked out the flagship and then spotted the landing bay outlined in subtle lights. He set up his approach, aiming not at the hatch but at where it would be when he was ready to dock with it.

As he approached, the main hatch opened and the interior appeared glowing dimly. He aimed at the lights on the far wall, bringing his ship in slowly. He crossed the threshold and touched down on the deck. As he did, he cut the main power switches and then steered toward the parking area where he shut down the engine. He glanced over his shoulder as the turbine wound down and saw the outer hatch begin to close though the interior lights kept flashing red, telling him that there was no oxygen on the deck.

He sat for a moment and watched as the lights changed to amber and finally to green. As he popped the hatch to climb out of the scout, he noticed a group was coming across the deck toward him. They didn't seem to be very happy.

As he straightened up, he saw the Colonel and two of his staff officers appear. Price saluted sharply and said, "We need to talk."

"Captain, what in the hell do you think you're doing? No

one authorized your flight or the landing on Bolton's Planet.''

"Yes, sir," agreed Price. "But I have it, Colonel. The whole story." He looked at the three officers, saw that they were unimpressed. He said, "Tell me one thing. Has everyone on the landing team disappeared yet?''

"They have not disappeared," said the Colonel. "A number of them are in the hospital but we know where they are. They are out of communication with us, but they have not disappeared.''

"There is something else going on there, Colonel. Our people are not sick. They're being brainwashed." He glanced around at each of the staff officers and saw that they were not believing what he told them. To buy time, he asked, "Should we be talking about this here?''

"Captain, I'm trying to decide if I should arrest you immediately for stealing that scout ship, for violating your orders, for a dozen different unlawful acts committed on Bolton's Planet.''

"Colonel, that's not important now." He lowered his voice and said, "Lieutenant Hamstein is dead.''

"What?''

"Local police killed her for leaving their medicenter with me." Price knew that wasn't quite right but at the moment he didn't care. Besides, by the time anyone found out the absolute truth of what happened, he would have the chance to explain the situation to them.

"All right, Captain," said the Colonel, "we're going to my conference room now. I want a full report.''

"Yes, sir. Might I suggest that we alert the Marines for a rescue mission?''

"I'll take that under advisement. Let's go.''

Price followed him out of the landing bay. He hoped that he could make his case before someone arrested him.

Coollege awoke and found herself again strapped to her cot. She no longer felt as if she had to escape. At least not right at that moment. Instead, she wanted to stay right where she was. She was relaxed and feeling good. She glanced toward the door as it opened.

White entered, followed by Sister Susan. White, noticing the leather straps, asked, "Does she need to be restrained?"

"How do you feel?" asked Sister Susan. She moved forward and looked down at Coollege.

"Much better."

"Well, let me talk to the doctor," Sister Susan said to White, "and we'll see what we can do about getting those straps removed."

"I would appreciate it," said Coollege.

White dragged a chair over, closer to the cot, and sat down. He patted her hand. "You're looking very good."

"Thank you," said Coollege. She tugged at the straps. "I would really like to get these removed."

The doctor pushed open the door and said, "Are we having a party in here?"

"Sorry, Doctor," said Sister Susan. "We were just trying to cheer up the patient."

The doctor bent over her, looked deep into her eyes, felt her pulse. He straightened up and studied her. "Are we feeling better?"

"I'm feeling much better today."

"I think," said the doctor, "that another day of treatment is necessary. We'll talk in the morning."

"I would really like to use the bathroom," said Coollege. "I really don't want to have a nurse bring me a bedpan and have her adjust it while I'm tied down like this. It's . . . just embarrassing."

"All right," said the doctor. He unfastened one of the wrist restraints and then attacked the one around the right ankle. "If you don't behave yourself, you'll find yourself tied down here again."

Coollege unhooked the other restraint and sat up. When her other ankle was unfastened, she swung her legs around and sat on the edge of the bed. "You don't know how uncomfortable that can get. It makes it seem like such a luxury to lay on my side or my stomach.''

''Your behavior has dictated the situation,'' said the doctor sternly.

''I'll be on my best behavior.'' She stood up and swayed once, reaching out to steady herself. ''It feels so good to be able to stand.'' She took a step forward, hesitated, then walked into the bathroom.

It was a small room with a toilet, sink, and shower. There was a wooden door that led to a small closet. She opened that but there was no escape through it. A medicenter robe hung in it along with a set of white towels.

She searched the medicine cabinet but there was nothing there to use as a weapon. She leaned back, against the sink, her arms folded. The only thing she could do was make a break for the door and try to get out of the medicenter before they could stop her. That didn't get her out of the city and she would probably be caught within minutes.

There was nothing she could do at the moment. And it seemed that White was now on the other side. He was there, all smiles, patting Sister Susan on the shoulder, as if they were friends from the distant past. It seemed that he had been converted.

Finally she opened the door and walked back to her cot. She sat down on it, looked up at the doctor, and said, ''The restraints aren't necessary.''

The doctor rubbed his chin and said, ''I suppose that we can leave them off for the morning. You're scheduled for a treatment this afternoon.''

She looked right into the doctor's eyes and said, ''Do I have to wait until this afternoon?''

He grinned broadly and said, ''I'm afraid so.'' He turned his attention to Sister Susan. ''You'll be here the rest of the morning?''

''If you feel it necessary.''

''Then that settles it,'' said the doctor. ''I'll continue my rounds. I'll see you right after lunch.''

"Yes, Doctor."

When the doctor left the room, Sister Susan said, "Things are beginning to look up."

Coollege knew what she meant. The treatments were beginning to work. Everyone was beginning to slip to the side of those on Bolton's Planet.

"Do you think I might be able to walk outside this morning?" asked Coollege.

"That might be pushing things a little," said Sister Susan. "Probably tomorrow."

Coollege nodded but knew that tomorrow would be too late. She was fighting to maintain her personality, her beliefs, in spite of the drugs she had been given. Another treatment might push her over the edge. She'd have to get out of that somehow.

"Tomorrow," she said, smiling. She hoped they believed her new attitude.

CHAPTER

20

Price told his story quickly and completely, showing the few pieces of visual evidence that he had been able to obtain. He pointed out that everyone in the landing party was out of touch with the fleet, that Coollege had disappeared, and that Hamstein and Wilcox had been shot down. He then told them that Hamstein had been killed by the local police as the two of them tried to escape.

The Colonel sat quietly listening and when Price finished, he asked, "Why did you make the unauthorized flight to the planet's surface?"

Price was surprised by the question. It ignored the information that he had just given them. It ignored the disappearance of everyone and the fact that the governmental officials of Bolton's Planet were refusing to answer questions about the landing team, Lieutenant Coollege, or the ship that had been shot down.

"Well?" asked the Colonel.

"I was worried about a leak in our organization," said Price quietly. "It seemed that those on the planet's surface knew everything about our operations and what we were doing here. That's the only way they could have detected and then shot down Hamstein. They had prior knowledge."

"That doesn't explain the unauthorized flight."

Price shook his head in disbelief. "Yes, sir, it does. I took the scout ship because I didn't want to telegraph the move to the enemy . . ."

"There is no enemy on the planet at the moment," said the Colonel sharply.

"Yes, sir," snapped Price. "It might appear that way but they are sure as hell acting like it."

"You said that there are spies in our organization. Do you know who they are?"

"No, sir."

"Isn't that the job of military intelligence? Shouldn't you be trying to determine where the leak is rather than making unauthorized flights to the planet and engaging in activities that result in the deaths of their citizens and our soldiers?"

"Finding the spy is the function of counterintelligence," said Price.

"Did you inform them of your suspicions?" asked the Colonel. "Did you tell anyone of your suspicions?"

"No, sir. I felt that my job required that I learn as much as I could about the situation on the ground. Because of my suspicions, I wanted to run the operation as quietly as possible. That's why I made the flight, feeling that once I returned and explained the situation, the flight would then be retroactively authorized."

"Captain, I'm not sure that I completely approve of your actions here, but I understand the rationale behind them. Because of that, I'm going to now authorize your flight. You need not worry about that any longer."

Price was relieved. "Thank you, sir."

"Now, moving on to other things, more important things. Are you sure that our missing people are being held in the medicenter?"

"I found Hamstein there and she confirmed that others were there as well."

"All of them?"

"My best . . . estimate." He grinned. He'd nearly said guess. "My best estimate is that all are currently held there. Although I didn't see them. We know, based on information received from the planet, that Colonel White is at the medicenter as well. I think we can take that as confirmation that Hamstein was right about it."

"You've been in the medicenter?"

"Yes, sir. I managed to see the whole thing. I believe that we can get a good map of New Washington with the medicenter marked on it."

"How many people do you think we'll need to overrun the medicenter?"

The question surprised Price, just as the close questioning about his flight surprised him. He thought about it and then asked, "Are you planning to just raid it or do you want to hold it?"

"Just a quick in and out raid. I want to get our people out and then evacuate the assault forces."

"I would think a company would be sufficient. They'd need to block all exits and move in rapidly. I think the police would respond but they couldn't mount a successful counterattack. We'd have thirty to forty minutes before there would be any kind of coordinated response. This presupposes that we'd have sufficient air cover."

"How long before you could have a briefing put together for the battle staff?"

"An hour. I need to call up the computer files on the capital and create the floor plans of the medicenter."

"You have your hour."

"Colonel, there is one thing that I need to say. We must limit the access to this information. I still think we've got someone hiding here who could provide information to the . . . enemy."

"I'm fully aware of the need for security. You may rest

assured that the circulation of the information will not exceed those who need to know.''

"Yes, sir.''

"You have work to do.''

Price stood up and saluted. "Thank you, Colonel.''

Price returned to the intelligence office, turned on the computers, and then sat back. He stared at the blank screen and thought about the problem. Not the design of the medicenter, but the possibility that there was a spy on the ship. Someone who was sending information to Bolton's Planet.

The problem shouldn't be that hard to solve. All he had to do was isolate the names of the people who would have had access to the data and then search for a connection between that person and Bolton's Planet.

He turned to the keyboard and typed in a series of short commands. He was searching for the distribution list for the data that had obviously been leaked, the individuals with access to the data through job assignments, and then anyone else who might have learned of the various missions. With the computer printing out that list, he then asked for anyone with ties to Bolton's Planet, whether it was their place of birth, had relatives who might have immigrated to it, or even those who had visited the planet anytime in the last several years. With that complete, he asked the computer to review both lists and provide the names of anyone who appeared on both lists.

The computer displayed three names. Price read them and shook his head. "It can't be that easy."

He got a printout of the three names and then wiped the computer's memory of the search. He wanted to leave no trace for the spy to find.

Satisfied with that, he turned his attention to the other problems. He prepared a number of maps showing New Washington, the location of the medicenter and other buildings that had been identified during his recon, and other relevant information that was available. That finished, he made a map of the medicenter itself, using his own observations. He tried to check it with area charts and blueprints but the computer didn't have access to all the data he wanted.

Finished, he asked for multiple printouts on various sizes to be distributed to the officers who would be making the assault. He also had the computer generate a small booklet that contained the pictures and biographies of all the missing people. He left the picture and bio of Hamstein out. They wouldn't be finding her.

The ICS chimed and Price reached over to punch a button. The regiment's chief of staff appeared. "We're ready in the conference room."

"Thank you. I'll be right there."

Price gathered his material, including the names of the three who could be the spy. He left the office, locking the hatch as he did. He then walked to the conference room, surprised to find an armed guard stationed outside it. That was a throwback to the days on Earth when there was a real possibility that a spy could get close enough to listen in. The guard was there to impress the staff with the importance of the meeting.

As the guard nodded to him, telling him to pass because he was on the access list and had been recognized, Price realized that the guard might be necessary. He had just completed making a list with the names of the spy on it.

When he entered the conference room, he saw that the Colonel was at the head of the table, his chief of staff at the first position on the right, his operations officer opposite on the left, and three company officers who would be leading the assault sitting there. The pilots of the assault craft would be briefed later since their job was only to find the right building and land where they were told to land.

Price set his material on the table and pulled out his chair. He glanced at the Colonel and waited.

"Gentlemen and ladies, we're about to commit an act of

war. We are about to put an armed force on the ground on a sovereign planet, attacking one of their facilities. Our justification is to obtain the return of a number of our people being held against their will. If there is anyone here who has a moral objection to this mission, then leave now."

No one moved. The Colonel grinned. "That's good because it would have ended your career. There is nothing wrong with the protection of our people and if you believed otherwise, then you are in the wrong occupation." He gestured toward Price. "You may take over now, Captain."

"Thank you, Colonel." Price stood up and then outlined the situation as it stood. He showed the maps of the city and the building, pointed out the exits and possible escape routes. He noted where the police buildings were, the air and spaceports in relation to the medicenter, the various residence halls, streets, and other lines of communications. He provided, based on his personal observations and the various reference works, both classified and unclassified, a complete picture of the city. He then made recommendations for the assault, based on his observations and his training early in his career as an infantry officer.

When he finished, the Colonel took over again. He pointed at the map of the medicenter and asked, "They could escape from the roof?"

"I'm more concerned with someone landing a reinforcement party on the roof," said Price. "It's certainly large enough for a couple of choppers, and there isn't much on the roof to prevent a landing. A squad with automatic weapons and personal antiaircraft missiles could hold it for fifteen or twenty minutes easily, however."

"Good point."

"If we try to cover all the exits and still have people on the roof, our force is going to be cut way down," said the company commander.

"One man or woman on each door, inside the medicenter, would be able to cover it. Radio communications between those people and the main body so that you can respond to any threat. And a single squad on the roof," said Price.

"Infantry tactics dictate that we never split our force in hostile territory."

"No," roared the Colonel, slamming a hand to the tabletop. "I hate it when only part of a doctrine is quoted. You do not split your forces in hostile territory until the size and distribution of the enemy forces is known. We have that knowledge. Dividing your team will not be a problem."

"Yes, sir."

Price said, "At most, you'll come up against the police force. They are well trained, but I don't think they have much experience against an armed enemy. If they've run up against a mob, that mob is unarmed and probably not coordinated. But they are professionals, trained in the use of their firearms. Don't underestimate them."

"How large is the police force?"

"The entire city has about three thousand officers. Not all will be on duty when we hit. The remainder will be scattered throughout the city. At most, they might be able to respond, quickly, with about one thousand."

"Which puts the odds at five to one for them," said the operations officer.

"We'll have air cover," said the Colonel, "and we should have a firepower advantage. That will even the odds quite a bit for us."

The company commander stood up and twisted the map of the medicenter around. "Looks like there are, what, three hundred rooms in this building. It's going to take us a while to clear them."

"Once you're down, searching for our people, and they realize you're there, I'm sure they will find you," said the Colonel.

"You won't have to search every room," said Price. "And you can call out, asking our people to step into the hallway."

The young officer studied the map carefully. "I guess we could clear it in fifteen minutes."

"Then everyone up to the roof for evacuation," said the Colonel. "It'll be a piece of cake."

"Yes, sir," said the company commander. "A piece of cake. When do we hit the field?"

"As soon as we can get your company formed and briefed. Captain Price, you will accompany them into the field and answer any questions that might come up as the force is deployed."

"Am I to take that to mean that I will disembark with them on the planet's surface?"

"You may interpret your orders as you see fit but I don't want these people to be left high and dry."

"Yes, sir."

The Colonel looked at them one last time. "Twenty-four hours from now, this will all be over."

Price didn't like the way the Colonel had said that but knew he was right. In twenty-four hours he would be back on the ship. He hoped.

CHAPTER

21

The assault force had joined in the shuttle bay, standing in three long rows, separated by platoon breaks. They wore dark green uniforms that would absorb the beams of lasers, could deflect bullets to some extent, and that were fire resistant. It increased the survivability of each of the soldiers to some extent.

Each held a rifle and wore a pistol in a holster. Certain people had larger weapons, designated as squad weapons. They could blast through a wall, burn a helicopter out of the air, or punch through the armor of a tank. One squad had antiaircraft weapons. They would deploy to the roof to protect it and keep it clear so that their rescue craft could land when the time came for the evacuation.

Price was dressed the same as the other soldiers but only carried a pistol for personal protection. He found the company commander standing off to one side and walked up to him. "You ready?"

"As ready as I'll ever be," said Captain Hawn. "There

anything else that I should know about this before we hit the planet?''

"Shouldn't be any resistance in the medicenter," said Price. "You hurry and we might get out before the police have a chance to respond."

"I hope so."

One of the sergeants appeared, saluted, and said, "We're ready to load, sir."

"Go ahead."

There were four ships to be loaded. The soldiers lined up near the hatches and began to enter. They moved quickly and in minutes had disappeared. The officers and top NCOs followed them into the shuttles.

"You'll be coming with me?" asked Hawn.

"Right behind you."

They walked to the lead ship. Hawn ducked and entered. The interior was dim, the soldiers sitting in rows facing to the rear. The three seats closest to the hatch were vacant, left for Hawn and his staff.

"You stay right here," said Hawn.

"What's the plan once we reach the ground?"

"We evacuate the ship using all the exits, including the emergency ones. Last soldier out shuts it and the ship lifts off to orbit about twenty, thirty thousand feet above the ground. We issue the recall and they pick us up."

Price sat down and buckled himself in using the seat belt and shoulder harness. He tugged it tight and watched as the hatch was closed by one of the deck crew. It became even darker inside until a series of red lights came on.

The engines began to wind up and the ship vibrated with the power. There were no windows so Price couldn't see what was happening outside the ship.

"Here we go," said a voice in the back.

Hawn dropped into his seat and leaned over closer and said, "Someone always has to say that."

"I was waiting for someone to say, 'This is it.'"

"Yeah, they seem to be hung up on the clichés. Just once I'd like to hear something original," said Hawn.

They began to slide forward and Hawn quickly buckled himself in. He then held out a hand and said, "Let me see that map once again."

Price handed it over, aware that they were picking up speed. The sound from the engines was growing, filling the interior of the shuttle, making it difficult to talk.

Hawn twisted the map around. He held it up, close to his eyes. There was nothing that he hadn't seen before. The plan looked solid.

"I guess we're set," said Hawn.

"I hope so," said Price, "since we're on the way."

Price thought that he had dozed on the flight in. It seemed that they had gotten to Bolton's Planet too fast. He twisted around and looked at the soldiers behind him. They looked ready. They held their weapons in their hands. They had pulled the visors down on their helmets. They had pulled on their gloves to protect their hands.

Hawn had done the same and now looked like something from another world. The silver of the visor, designed to reflect beamed weapons, sparkled red in the cabin's dim light.

"I'll warn you," said Hawn. "Unfasten your belts and leap clear of the hatch. Follow me once we get into the medicenter. Stay close."

"I'll follow you in, but I'm going after Lieutenant Coollege. She's in there somewhere."

Hawn turned and said, "Corporal Watson, Private McCloskey, you stick with Captain Price."

"Yes, sir."

"One minute to touchdown," said a voice over the PA system. "One minute."

Hawn checked his weapon, fingered the safety to make sure it was still on, and then stared at the hatch.

"Thirty seconds."

One of the crewmen moved to the hatch and crouched near it. He wore a long bungee cord and held on to a handle fastened to the bulkhead.

"Fifteen."

Hawn unfastened his harness. "Remember. Out the hatch and out of the way."

"Got it."

The nose came up suddenly and they were forced down into the seats. Price fought to take a breath and tried to shift forward. The nose dropped and they settled to the ground. As they touched down, the crewman spun a wheel and the hatch irised open quickly.

One of the sergeants was up on his feet yelling, "Go! Go! Go!"

Price jumped into the line, leapt through the hatch, and then dived to the right, near the tail of the shuttle. He watched as the soldiers fanned out, heading to the four exits that were closest to them.

The other shuttles fell out of the sky, taking positions around the medicenter, surrounding it, and blocking the other exits. The soldiers swarmed out, taking what cover they could find, watching the building.

Hawn ran by Price, heading for the closest door. Price joined him, the soldiers following in behind them. Hawn leapt through the door, rolled to his right, and came up facing the startled people inside.

"Hands up," said Hawn. "No one will get hurt." He glanced back at two of his soldiers and ordered them, "Take these people into a room and guard them."

"Yes, sir."

"Second floor," said Price.

"Right behind you," said Hawn.

They ran to the escalator. Other soldiers had already secured it, entering through the front doors. Nurses, doctors, technicians, stood along a wall, hands behind their heads, two soldiers guarding them.

"Holding point is down the hallway," said Hawn. "Take them there."

Price and the two soldiers assigned to him ran up the escalator. A nurse saw them and dropped the tray she held. It clattered to the floor. A man appeared from his room, looked at the soldiers, and disappeared into the interior.

Hawn and half a dozen more soldiers fanned out on the floor. "Round up the staff and hold them at the nurse's station."

"Yes, sir."

Price ran down the hall, looking right and left, stopping only to push open a door. When he didn't recognize the occupant, he ran on.

Near the end of the hall, he found White. The Colonel was sitting up in his bed, one of the locals sitting with him. Price entered the room, his pistol drawn, the two others standing behind him like guards.

White, clearly startled, demanded, "What in the hell is going on here?"

"We've come to free you, Colonel," said Price.

"Free me from what?"

"Colonel," said Price, "we're all going back to the fleet now."

"No, Captain, we are not. I'm staying here and finishing my regimen of treatments."

The words of Hamstein rang in his ears. She'd talked of treatments, too. She had been in the medicenter and hadn't wanted to leave.

"Sir," said Price, "your entire landing team disappeared. We've been sent to recover them."

"Of all the balled-up nonsense. All you had to do was ask. There is no reason to burst in here with rifles and pistols like common criminals."

"Then you'll come along?" said Price.

"Hell, no. I'm staying right here."

"Private McCloskey," said Price, "you will remain here with the Colonel."

"Yes, sir.

"What about the woman?" he asked.

"She stays here too." Price glanced at her. "Just remain calm and no one will get hurt. All we want is to get our people out of here."

"Our police will be here in a few minutes and then you'll see what a real fighting force can do," said the woman.

"I hope you're wrong," said Price. "The last thing we want is bloodshed."

"Get out now and there won't be any," she said.

"Captain, I don't know where you got your orders, but I'm going to take this up with the general as soon as I'm discharged from this facility . . ."

"Yes, sir," said Price, interrupting. "I don't have time to argue the point." To Watson, he said, "Let's get moving."

As they stepped into the hall, Price saw Hawn. "Found the Colonel. Left McCloskey with him."

"Got two others at the far end," said Hawn.

"What about Coollege?"

"Haven't seen her."

Price nodded and said, "I'm going up to the next floor." He turned and started toward the steps but then stopped. "You'd better have someone stay with our people . . ."

"That's already been done."

"Good." Price slapped Watson on the chest and they both ran for the fire stairs.

When they reached the third level, they saw half a dozen of the landing team standing in the hallway with soldiers near them. Another group of soldiers were guarding the medicenter staff at the station near the escalator.

"Anyone seen Coollege?" he shouted.

"No, sir."

"Fourth floor," he said to Watson.

They ran up to the fourth floor. As he burst from the stairwell, he saw Coollege standing near one of the rooms. She was wearing a medicenter gown and looked as if she hadn't slept in several days.

Price ran toward her. "Hey, Jackknife. What the hell are you doing here?"

"Tree! About time you arrived. Get me the hell out of here before they wash my brain."

"You got any real clothes?"

"In my room."

"Climb into them and we'll head for the roof. Exfiltration will be made from there."

"Another day or so and they'd have had me," she said. "Almost."

"It's okay. We're recovering the landing team and getting out."

Without another word, she disappeared into the room. Price stood near the door. He peeled off his helmet and wiped the sweat from his face. The medicenter was air-conditioned but he hadn't noticed.

"That it, sir?" asked Watson.

"For me, yes."

Coollege reappeared, tugging at one of the zippers. "You found Rocky yet?"

"We'll get him," said Price. "Let's head up to the roof. I want to be on the first ship out of here."

Together they walked toward the escalator and rode it up to the top floor. The scene there was the same that they had seen on each of the others. The soldiers guarding the medicenter staff at the main station, some patients in the hallway, and a knot of soldiers around the members of the landing team.

They exited onto the roof and found the soldiers there spread out in a defensive pattern to defeat an air assault on the position. The sergeant in charge rushed over but didn't salute.

"We're set here, sir."

"I think we've about gotten the medicenter cleared. They'll be coming up here in a few minutes."

"Should I recall the shuttles?"

"Let's wait for Captain Hawn to issue that order. It may take him a few more minutes to get everything finished."

"Yes, sir."

Price began to relax then. They had made it through the medicenter without a shot being fired. They'd located the landing team and were getting them up to the roof. Fifteen minutes had elapsed from the moment he'd rushed through the doors until he reached the roof. The mission had gone off exactly as it had been planned.

More of the assault force began to arrive. They fanned out, taking up positions next to the squad already there, strengthening those positions. They scanned the skies, searching for the police, but saw nothing other than a couple of high-flying birds.

Coollege sat down and hugged her knees. In a quiet voice, she said, "You don't know what they were doing to us. You just don't know."

"When we get back, you can tell me."

"It was so hard to resist . . . if it hadn't been for the counterintelligence training, I'd have never made it. They'd have gotten me too."

"Which explains White and the others."

"You can't blame them," said Coollege. "The system is very sophisticated . . . I was . . ."

"It's okay, Jackknife," said Price. "We'll get it all when we get to the fleet."

The far door burst open and Hawn ran out. He sprinted to the edge of the roof and looked down on the north side and then charged across to the south. He found the sergeant who had been in command of the antiaircraft squad.

"You see anything?"

"No, sir. Quiet as a church up here. Nothing to see. Nothing at all."

Hawn saw Price and ran over to him. "How long you been up here?"

"Few minutes."

"You see anything?"

"No. What in the hell is going on?"

He hitchhiked a thumb. "We've got a company moving in on us. Carefully. They know what they're doing."

"Then let's get the shuttles down here and get the hell out before anything goes wrong."

"Sergeant. Issue the recall order."

"Yes, sir."

Hawn ducked and made his way to the edge of the roof, looking down. "Now, if they'll just hold off until the shuttles arrive, we'll be okay."

It was then that a line of black-clad police appeared, running for the medicenter. The counterattack had begun.

CHAPTER

22

White stood in the hallway, watching as the soldiers circulated. He was beginning to get angry. There was no reason for them to be there, violating a half-dozen inter-planetary agreements and treaties. Sister Susan stood erect, her arms folded. It was obvious that she was angry about the armed intrusion.

"I'll get to the bottom of this," White promised her angrily. "I don't know what the hell they're thinking but we'll get to the bottom of this."

"We will lodge a formal protest just as soon as we're allowed to leave the medicenter."

White left his room and moved toward the nurse's station. "Sergeant," he called to the highest-ranking soldier he saw, "why are the locals being held here?"

The sergeant didn't recognize White and since he wore only the medicenter gown and not a uniform, the sergeant wasn't impressed. "Who are you?"

"Colonel White, in command of the landing team."

"Well, Colonel," said the sergeant, sounding as if he

didn't believe White, "my orders are to hold everyone in the building until we can begin our exfiltration."

"Sister Susan," said White, pointing to the woman, "will be allowed to leave now."

"No, sir. She will stay right where she is until we are cleared from the area. Those are my orders and I will not deviate from them."

"I outrank you, Sergeant, and I am giving you new orders. If you fail to obey them, I will have you arrested on our return to the fleet."

The sergeant turned his back and said, "Someone put this man back with the others."

"Sure, Sarge."

White stood still, the color drained from his face. He was so angry that he couldn't speak. The words just wouldn't form. He whirled finally and stomped back to where Sister Susan waited for him.

"Don't worry," she said, "our police will be here in a few minutes and that will be the end of it."

"I just don't understand this," he said finally, his rage almost under control. "I don't understand it at all."

Crouching at the edge of the roof, Hawn watched as the line of police worked to get closer to the medicenter. He tried to count them but lost track. All were armed with rifles. There didn't seem to be any larger weapons with them.

"I think we can hold them," said Hawn to Price. He used the radio, "Two one, you've got company coming your way. Let's look alive."

"Roger. We've got them spotted."

"You are cleared to fire when you are ready. It is not necessary to give them the first shot."

"Roger that."

Hawn sat back and took a deep breath. He turned toward the sergeant. "I think you'd better whistle up the air support and get them into position."

"Yes, sir."

"What about the exfiltration?" asked Price.

"We'll get that arranged quickly."

There was a sudden burst of firing. One weapon, on full auto, firing into the medicenter. The rounds shattered glass and whined off the stone.

"That's not one of ours," said Hawn.

Price looked over the edge of the roof and saw two police officers behind a bench firing at the front door of the medicenter. Bright beams flashed from inside, hitting the bench, destroying it. The machine gunners scrambled away, running for safety.

"That's the way to do it," said Hawn. "Drive them back without hurting anyone."

Shooting erupted from around the perimeter, some of it directed at the roof. Bits of stone and brick flew off. One of the guy wires of an attenna began to glow and then snapped. A soldier was hit by a beam, dodged to the right, and tripped, falling.

"I'm okay," he said, holding up a hand.

"Time to get out now," said Price.

"I think you're right." Hawn crawled to the rear and found the sergeant. "Exfiltration sequence now."

"Yes, sir."

"Two one, you've got to hold the ground floor for ten to fifteen minutes."

"Roger that."

"Two three, begin to bring your people up to the roof."

"What about the locals?"

"Shit. Hold them at the station. Two people to guard. The rest of you get up here."

"Yes, sir."

Firing from below increased. Another old-fashioned machine gun began to hammer, the slugs raking the top of the building, snapping overhead. Beams flashed and vanished. The antenna was hit again and the top exploded, showering bits of metal and glass over the rooftop.

Hawn worked his way back to the edge of the roof and saw a line of police surge forward. They ran from the cover of other buildings, dodging right and left, using the little cover from benches, bushes, and lampposts. They fired as they ran, their weapons flashing, the beams and bullets hitting the medicenter but doing no real damage.

As the line surged toward them, the soldiers inside the medicenter opened fire, at first putting the rounds and the beams into the ground in front of the assault. When that failed to stop it, they began to aim at the enemy. Then officers began dropping from the line. Just one or two, but as the others continued, shouting and shooting, more of the soldiers shot down into the crowd. More of the enemy fell, the open area suddenly littered with the dead and injured of the police force.

"Shit," said Hawn again. "I didn't want a fight." He pushed himself from the edge of the roof and stood. To the sergeant, he said, "You are responsible for keeping the roof clear. The shuttle lands, you get it loaded and off. That's all you have to do."

"Yes, sir."

"Price."

"Yeah."

"You want to help us or you just interested in getting out of here?"

"What do you need?"

"Come with me."

Coollege was sitting back, away from the edge of the roof. When Price looked at her, she said, "Go. I can get on the shuttle by myself."

"Let's go," said Hawn.

They ran down toward the door and then down the steps. They passed a number of soldiers heading on up. A couple of people were wearing medicenter gowns but didn't look pleased with the situation. They were following the soldiers reluctantly.

As they reached the sixth floor, they heard more firing

coming from the right. Hawn pointed and said, ''See what you can do over there. I'm going down to the ground floor. We want an orderly withdrawal.''

''Got it,'' said Price.

Hawn ran for the escalator and started down. He hoped that he could get everyone out before the situation got desperate.

Price found a group of soldiers in the stairwell. Part of one wall had crumbled and they were shooting down at the police officers, holding them at bay. One of the soldiers lay on the floor, blood pooling under the body. Someone had pulled the helmet off the woman. Her skin was flat white, waxy-looking, as if she had been created from local materials. It was obvious that she was dead.

''They're coming up the stairs,'' said one man.

''How do you know that they're not our people?'' asked Price.

''They were shooting at us.''

Price nodded and checked his pistol again. ''Two men, come with me.''

''Right behind you, Captain,'' said a voice.

Price turned and saw Watson. ''I thought you were on the roof.''

''Captain Hawn said to stick with you, sir.''

''Okay. One other.''

''Right here,'' said a voice.

''Then let's go. The rest of you, hold your fire on the stairs until we've cleared out. Either I'll order it, or one of these men. No one else.''

''Yes, sir.''

Price took a deep breath, and stepped over the threshold. With his back against the wall, he began the descent. He leaned forward, trying to see down but the stairs were empty. The sound of the firing covered any noise he made. Of course, it covered that by the enemy.

He reached the landing and held up a hand. Rubble from

the wall littered the stairs. A body was crumpled on the next landing. A pistol was near one hand. Blood stained the floor and part of the wall.

Price waved and started down, listening carefully but hearing only the heavy hammering of the machine guns being used outside by the locals. A window, set high on a wall, shattered, glass splattering them all.

Price crouched near the body and touched the throat but there was no pulse. He picked up the pistol and shoved it into a pocket. As he stepped over the dead man, the door below opened and two police officers leapt through. Price didn't hesitate. He fired, pulling his trigger fast. The sounds of the shots echoed in the confined space.

One of the officers fell to his side, but kept firing, the bullets striking the wall near Price. They whined off, hitting the rail or the steps. He rolled to his back and tried to reload as his partner opened fire.

The muzzle flashes strobed in the stairwell. Price fired into the center of them. The man grunted suddenly and sat down. He dropped his weapon and folded over. Price jumped to the right, down two steps, and aimed at the first man, but he had dropped his pistol and was lying still.

"You hit, Captain?" asked Watson.

"I'm fine. Coming back up."

"Yes, sir."

Price retreated rapidly, suddenly aware that his hands were shaking. He lifted his hand and wiped the sweat from his face. He reached the landing and stopped, sinking to one knee. He realized that the firefight had taken under ten seconds. If he hadn't caught them by surprise, they would have killed him. He wondered how they had gotten to the fifth floor.

White ducked when the first shots were fired, but he was in an inside hallway, safe from the firefight raging below him. Instead, he watched as the soldiers fanned out, guard-

ing the escalator and both ends of the hallway. Only two
watched the locals corraled at the nurse's station.

To Sister Susan he said, "You wait right here. I'm going
to end this crap right now."

He walked down the hallway and said to the closest
soldier, "I'm going to take these people out of here now.
Take out the noncombatants."

"No, sir."

White's right hand shot out and grabbed the shirt of the
man. He stepped in close, inside the arc of the barrel of the
man's weapon, and struck him in the chest, throat, and
bridge of the nose in rapid succession. As the soldier
sagged, White grabbed the rifle and reversed it, pulling the
trigger. The beam stabbed out, touched the other soldier on
the arm, and then cut across his chest. He leapt back, tried
to fire, but White kept the beam steady on him. The soldier
groaned in sudden pain and slumped to the floor.

"Come on," yelled White. "Let's get out of here."

Sister Susan ran down the hallway and headed toward the
escalator. White followed her, protecting her back. Someone fired at him, the beam singeing his hair. He shot back
and the soldier dived for cover.

They ran down the escalator, reaching the first floor. The
soldiers there were barricaded in front of the door and were
hiding near the windows. Most of the glass in the windows
had been shattered and lay scattered on the floor, flashing in
the late-afternoon sun.

One of the soldiers whirled and then lowered his weapon
when he recognized White. "Colonel. You need to get back
up to the roof. Exfiltration will begin in a moment or two."

A burst of machine-gun fire ripped through the door. The
bullets hammered at the ceiling, knocking chunks from it.
One of the soldiers screamed, clutched at his chest, and fell
to the floor.

"Colonel."

"No. I need to get some of these people out of here right
now."

"No, sir. Everyone stays until we can get clear."

"I will not tolerate the taking of hostages," roared White. "They will be freed immediately."

"Yes, sir. Please stay back. I don't want anyone hurt by accident."

"Let the police know what is happening in here," said White. "Right now."

"Yes, sir." The soldier turned and moved to the side of the door. He leaned around and shouted, "We're sending out some of the medicenter staff."

The answer was a long burst from a machine gun, tearing holes in the side of the entrance. Splinters flew. Shards of glass exploded.

"No good, Colonel."

"We're going out," said White. "Make no mistake about that."

Sister Susan, who had been standing behind him, touched his sleeve and whispered something to him. White nodded and said, "Let her talk to the police."

"No, sir. I can't do that."

"You can and will."

The soldier turned his back as if to say that the discussion was over. White fired from the hip. The beam touched the soldier low, in the small of the back. He jumped forward, as if to get away from the beam, but hit the wall and slipped to the floor dead.

"Get going," yelled White.

Another soldier opened fire. The beam touched White, setting his medicenter gown on fire. He screamed in sudden pain, and dropped his weapon, falling to his knees. Sister Susan picked it up and aimed at the soldier but was cut down, the beams of half a dozen weapons striking her.

White tried to get to his feet but failed. He fell forward and lay still. He couldn't figure out what had happened. As the world around him faded to black, he wondered why he had taken Sister Susan's side in the dispute. He should have been trying to reach the roof just as he had been told to by the young officers.

Hawn appeared from the side. He saw the bodies of White and Sister Susan but ignored them. He called out, "I want everyone to fall back on my order. We will form on the second floor, holding the escalator and the stairwells."

The soldiers fell back one at a time, running across the open lobby and then up the escalator. As they reached the second floor, they fanned out, taking up new defensive positions.

Hawn retreated to the stairwell and watched as the last of the soldiers deserted their posts on the ground floor. He had expected the police to rush forward, but apparently they hadn't realized what was happening.

Then, overhead, came a whoosh that sounded like a shuttle dropping from the sky and suddenly turning to climb out. A moment later there was an explosion in front of the medicenter. The close air support had finally arrived and was keeping the police pinned down.

Hawn realized that they now had their chance. He ran to the stairwell. "Get moving. Everyone, get moving. Head toward the roof." He heard the soldiers scrambling upward. He crouched in the doorway, watching the ground floor, but the police weren't coming. They were staying in position on the outside as if they believed they had the soldiers bottled up in the medicenter.

"We're cleared, sir."

"Right behind you." Hawn took the steps two at a time. When he reached the second floor, he used the radio. "Let's evacuate now. Everyone upstairs."

"What about the locals?"

"Leave them behind. Let's just get going."

"Roger that."

Hawn waited on the stairs, watching the hallway as the soldiers evacuated it, using the escalator to retreat to the third floor. Once his people had moved off, Hawn turned and ran up the stairs.

There he found two of his soldiers in a fight with part of the original landing team. Hawn ran from the stairwell, shouting, "What in the hell is going on here?"

One of the soldiers straightened and said, "They refuse to come with us."

"Why?"

"We belong here," said the woman. "There is no reason for us to return to the fleet."

"There is no room for debate. You're going with us and that's it."

"You can't enforce that order," said the woman.

"Sergeant, if they won't come peacefully, knock them out and drag them. I don't have time to screw around with this."

"Yes, sir!"

"You wouldn't . . ."

"Just try me," snapped Hawn. "We've got to move."

There was another rumbling explosion from outside. Hawn ducked instinctively as did the others. One man flattened himself on the floor.

"Come on," said Hawn. "We've got to get out."

Price retreated to the roof. He stayed close to the door, watching the stairwell. He heard the first of the shuttles swoop low and a moment later saw the explosion. He slipped to the edge of the roof. The police weren't advancing on the medicenter. They were holding back, as if waiting for reinforcements.

The first of the soldiers poured out the door and spread out on the roof. They began firing down, at the police officers below them. The police returned the fire. Bullets and beams tore at the top of the building.

"Keep pouring it down," yelled Price.

The sergeant appeared. "First of the exfiltration shuttles is on the way down."

"How many can it take?"

"Everyone on the roof."

"Tell Captain Hawn we need to get more of the people up here."

"Yes, sir."

Price crawled around and found Coollege stretched out on the roof, trying to keep out of the line of fire. "I want you to be on that first shuttle," said Price.

"I can take another one," said Coollege.

"No, we need to get you out of here. Once you're back, you need to begin preparing a statement about what happened down here. For the Colonel."

"Yes, sir."

"Shuttle coming in," yelled the sergeant.

Overhead the sky was split with the roar of the engines. Price turned to watch as the shuttle fell out of the nearly cloudless sky, flared as the nose came up, and then dropped toward the center of the roof.

Firing from the ground intensified. Beams flashed over them. Bullets hammered the edge of the roof, tearing away the stone. Something hit low and exploded, sending a cloud of dust and smoke up.

"Get on board," yelled the sergeant, waving an arm. "Move it. Move it."

Price jerked Coollege to her feet and pushed her toward the shuttle. "Hurry it up," he yelled.

She reached the open ramp, hesitated for an instant, and then disappeared inside. She was followed by others, including some of the people rescued on the lower floors. In seconds the doors were being closed and the shuttle was lifting off, hovering like a helicopter. There was a roar from the engines and the shuttle leapt into the air.

Now more people poured across the roof and as before took up positions along the edge, firing down at the police. From the right came the pounding of rotor blades.

"Got an aircraft coming at us."

"Antiaircraft crew!" yelled the sergeant.

Three soldiers ran to the right side of the roof. One of them handed the other a long, narrow tube that he lifted to his shoulder. Leaning his head against the aiming point, he said, "Activate."

The third soldier peeled a cover from the front and then the rear. He tapped the main man on the head and said, "You are activated."

"Got a lock."

"Ready to fire." He waited but there was no call for a delay. He pressed the trigger. With a roar and a flash of fire and smoke, the thin missile leapt from the tube. It corkscrewed out, toward the helicopter. The pilot saw the missile and turned, but it was too late. He tried to drop out of the sky but the missile turned with him, striking the chopper in the mast to the main rotor system. There was an orange fireball as the rotor blades went flying. The helicopter fell from the sky like a rock. It exploded on impact.

"Here they come," yelled one of the rooftop defenders.

Firing erupted all around the roof. More soldiers appeared, and finally Hawn was there with them. He crouched next to Price.

"We've got everyone off the floors."

"Shuttle coming in."

"Think we can get everyone on it?" asked Price.

"We've got fifty people here. Yeah. We can make it."

Below them the police were retreating again. The number of black shapes scattered over the ground was growing. They had been badly hurt in their attempts to storm the medicenter.

An instant later a hurricane force wind swept the top of the building and the shuttle, making a high-speed approach, suddenly dropped down. The rear hatch was open wide.

"Go!" shouted the sergeant.

Hawn stayed at his post firing down as the rest of his company ran for the shuttle. He kept shooting, even as it was clear that the police were going to make another assault.

Price finally grabbed his shoulder. "It's time for us to get out."

Hawn whirled and ran up the ramp, Price right beside him. The soldiers were strapping themselves in. Equipment had been dropped. One man had sprawled on the floor.

As they entered, the rear ramp was activated, closing rapidly. When it clicked shut, the shuttle lifted. Price was tossed to his right. He rolled to his belly and reached for the closest chair. He scrambled up and dropped into it as the engines roared. The shuttle was taking off.

For the moment, Price couldn't move, pinned to the chair by the force of gravity. He tried to reach for the seat belt, but didn't have the strength. He tried to breathe, tried to hold on, and prayed that the enemy would be unable to intercept.

And then, the pressure lessened and a voice came over the intercom. "We have cleared the atmosphere."

The shuttle erupted into cheering. The soldiers were pounding each other on the backs, dancing around, screaming their approval.

Hawn looked over at Price and said, "You got the information right."

Price laughed. "And you executed the rescue perfectly."

"We are good, aren't we."

Price could see no reason to disagree.

CHAPTER

23

When Price returned he spent three days putting together the information. He reviewed everything that Coollege had been through, interviewed those pulled from the medicenter, and worked with the fleet medical personnel who were trying to determine what drugs had been used.

Most of those from the landing team were still insisting that they be allowed to return to Bolton's Planet. It was where they belonged. Price didn't argue the point with them, he just kept asking his questions, putting down their answers as they gave them. He wasn't attempting to correlate the data, he was just trying to gather it.

When he finished, he told the Colonel he was ready to brief him. The Colonel assembled the staff and told Price that the floor was his.

"What we have," said Price by way of introduction, "is a society that has found a way of controlling the human impulses that have created so many problems for the rest of us. Through the use of drugs, brainwashing techniques that surpass anything practiced by anyone else, and a lifetime of conditioning, they have complete control over everyone. Those same techniques have been practiced on our landing team with good results, and I think that might be the key to this whole episode.''

''Meaning?'' asked the Colonel.

''I believe,'' said Price, ''that recently they found a way of creating the same results without the necessity of a lifetime of conditioning. In other words, through brainwashing and drugs, they can create the attitude in someone who has only just arrived on their planet.''

''This is important?'' asked the chief of staff.

''I think it is the key,'' said Price. ''Up until recently, they didn't have the success. They might have been able to convince some people, but the majority either wouldn't take the training, or rejected it as soon as they were away from the influence. That is why they were trying so hard to recover that cube we brought up. It demonstrated these new techniques and would allow us to develop counter-programming.''

Price stopped and laughed. ''Had they not tried that, we might never have gotten onto them. It provided the original clue.''

''How do you know?'' asked the Colonel. ''How do you know that the training isn't rejected once they have left the influence of the planet?''

''The spy on board our ship,'' said Price. ''He has been away from their influence for more than a month and he is still spying on us for them.''

''Who?'' asked the Colonel.

''Sergeant Stanley Nicks.''

''Oh, bullshit,'' said the chief of staff.

''Nicks is the one who pulled me out of the soup on the planet's surface. They believed that Nicks could recover the cube, not knowing that I had already passed it on to Stone. To make it look good, they tried to stop us. There was no real danger.''

''But . . .''

"I would suggest," said Price, "that Sergeant Nicks be placed under a doctor's care. He can be kept with the people from the landing team."

"What about Lieutenant Coollege?" asked the Colonel.

"I think that she, because of her training, was able to resist better. Had we not gotten down there when we did, we would have lost her. The same goes for Sergeant Stone. We got him out just in a nick of time."

"Recommendations?" asked the Colonel.

"First, I think that we need to broadcast a warning about Bolton's Planet. We need to alert everyone about this problem. That'll make it difficult for them to work this on anyone else. Then, we've got to learn who has visited Bolton's Planet in the last year and see if there is any reason to believe that they underwent this procedure."

"Can it be reversed?"

Price nodded. "That was the question that I asked our medical staff. If someone can be brainwashed, they can be unbrainwashed. Our doctors are convinced that the effects of the drugs are not permanent. There would have to be a way of giving boosters, if you will. That might be part of the conditioning process and then pills are supplied . . . I'm not sure how important all this is at the moment. I think what we need to do is get the message out."

The chief of staff said, "Colonel, are there any plans for retribution?"

"That's a good question." He was quiet for a minute or so. "Of course I'll have to take this up with the general, but I think the attitude is going to be that we have stopped their spread. We can warn the rest of the inhabited planets. That will probably be considered retribution enough."

Price spoke up again. "I think, given what we've learned, we can . . . overlook . . . Colonel White's behavior?"

"Oh, hell yes," said the Colonel. "He was killed in action. That'll be reflected in my report."

"That would go for the others as well," said the chief of staff.

The Colonel nodded and then asked, ''Is there anything else for us?''

Price shrugged. ''I think that's got it.''

''Then we're adjourned.''